An invigorating first novel … Cox's New York City has an off-hand, vibrant authenticity. It glitters and fumes. —*The Globe and Mail*

A startling debut novel … A distinctive coming-of-age story that poses thoughtful questions about the relationship between sex work and the creative process. A novel worth reading—for writers, whores, and everyone in between. —*Quill and Quire*

The character Jaeven is shrewd, calculating, and utterly captivating. Like a male Holly Golightly, he manages to twist everyone around his little finger with a wink and a smile—or maybe a smirk and a pout … *Shuck* is definitely a page-turner, which will surely make it a popular hit. —*Black Heart Magazine*

It's an exhilarating read; Cox has managed to make the seediness and occasional brutality of this world downright glamorous, recreating the New York of this time with eerie precision. —*Montreal Mirror*

In *Shuck*, these supposedly diametric opposites [of writer and whore] have met, made out and created a gay porn lovechild that references Dennis Cooper, JT LeRoy and the Marquis de Sade. —*Hour Magazine*

Shuck is unwavering in its portrayal of getting eaten slowly, but surely, by New York City's Big Apple … The diary entries are reminiscent of Jim Carroll's *Basketball Diaries*. It explores addiction, sexuality, and the part of New York City that isn't advertised. —*EDGE Publications*

Cox is a brilliant storyteller. He's able to reduce human emotion into hot shots of truth that singe the guts and set heads to shaking. Dirty and glorious, *Shuck* is definitely a fun read. —*NewPages.com*

FINALIST FOR A LAMBDA LITERARY AWARD

SHUCK

DANIEL ALLEN COX

ARSENAL PULP PRESS | VANCOUVER

ARSENAL PULP PRESS
Suite 200, 341 Water Street
Vancouver, BC
Canada V6B 1B8
arsenalpulp.com

The publisher gratefully acknowledges the support of the Canada Council for
the Arts and the British Columbia Arts Council for its publishing program, and
the Government of Canada through the Book Publishing Industry Development
Program and the Government of British Columbia through the Book Publishing
Tax Credit Program for its publishing activities.

This is a work of fiction. Any resemblance of characters to persons either living
or deceased is purely coincidental.

Book design by Shyla Seller
Editing by Brian Lam and Bethanne Grabham
Cover photograph: Joe Ovelman—"Paid 6," copyright Joe Ovelman, courtesy
Conner Contemporary Art, Washington, DC.
Author photo by Farah Khan, house9road47.com

Printed and bound in Canada on 100% post-consumer recycled paper

Library and Archives Canada Cataloguing in Publication

Cox, Daniel Allen
    Shuck / Daniel Allen Cox.

ISBN 978-1-55152-246-3

    I. Title.

PS8605.O934S58 2008   C813'.6   C2008-904091-0

I collect memorabilia and fossils
From all the places that you've haunted
And now I'm haunted

—"Spectres and Ghosts"
On Bodies, lyrics by Mark Harris

This book is dedicated to Coney Island and those who love it.

Part 1

I BET THAT RIGHT NOW, you're not listening to Duran Duran's "Ordinary World" in your Walkman, which means you won't understand a word I've written. You suck, but that's beside the point. Since you probably stole this notebook from me, I've already begun hunting you down, and there are two things you should know in case I attack you tiger-style from behind before you finish reading it:

1—I didn't do it to him on purpose.

B—You're never more than ten feet away from a guy who'll pay you to shuck your pants.

Test it out.

The guy standing behind you in line at the supermarket, look at what he's buying. They don't go together. See how he cruises you like a piece of fruit, and how disappointed he is when you don't give him the signal. He dumps the taco shells and ice cream in the magazine rack, and leaves empty-handed.

Customer two. The dude reading beside you on the subway,

nevermind. He's missed the whole last chapter, picturing your jeans in a funky pile at the foot of his bed. He knows he doesn't have to pay, but he wants to. He says nothing, waiting for the signal, reading your hands.

Do it. Hook your thumb in your belt loop more often, and you'll see what I mean. Even if you do it unprofessionally, they'll still swarm.

Jaeven Marshall, twenty-two.

I don't know what these guys see in me. They can easily buy a better trick just down the block.

My posture is atrocious, and my fingers are stained. I'm a mess, but they still come after me. My knees are like dowels come loose that I can't hammer back in. Sometimes they pay extra to lick the webs between my toes.

My balls are so tiny, I wonder if they've dropped yet. I have a lip ring that sometimes gets crusty, and I only shave when I find a disposable that doesn't look too iffy. I've got blue eyes, which some guys seem to trip on.

Welcome to my whatever.

A thundercloud crept toward me in the form of a car I recognized for its slow idle and hungry rumble—blue Pontiac with a stubbly leer.

A twenty attached to a hand waved out the window.

Five packs of cigarettes. Three decent meals. No matter how you sliced it, I needed that twenty.

I wasn't in the mood for a Red Taurus or a Lime Volkswagen because they usually got too kinky too fast, and not a Tiger-striped Jeep because rabbit-fuckers like that are too impatient and juvenile, and definitely not a Black Audi because that would just be asking for "God" trouble: power trips, etc. But a Blue Pontiac I could do. They usually wear a condom when I ask them to, when HIV is real enough in my mind.

I got in the car and did a cursory inspection of his genitals to check for any visible signs of escape wounds, claw marks left by other whores gone missing. When you fight back, there are only so many things you can reach for, and the trannies who own that West Side turf are famous for being vicious.

That's the thing. You're probably wondering what a fabulous rent boy like me is doing walking the West Side Highway when there are so many supermarkets around. You're wondering why I'm freezing my ass outside when there are plenty of guys who scribble down my pager number from the back of HX or Next magazines, and then beep me to take their erections away. Well, if you want to know the truth, a whore's got to do his market research to know who he's competing against. If the wolves can get better versions of me out on the street, my whole business model is in trouble.

So this guy, Blue Pontiac, did something unprofessional to me. It was nothing serious, like choosing a radio station without asking my preference, or making me kiss him without the presence of spearmint gum. Let's just say that he crossed me. It was nothing unforgivable, like asking me to call him by his name, and it was nothing stupid, like making me wait in the car while he ran to an ATM.

Let's just say that he was physically rude to me.

Now, I'm not a vengeful person, but I just couldn't help it. I was rather unprofessional with Blue Pontiac. It was nothing embarrassing, like laughing at his weenie, or recommending a crotch-to-head hair transplant. Let's just say that I stung him. It was nothing permanent, because I don't really know the meaning of the word.

I wonder what I'm going to do with his tax receipts. What toilet, what sewer, what shredder?

≡

My Fiorucci duffel bag makes for a great pillow, and it's also good for absorbing kicks, you know, the occasional ones you get from city monsters. My brown and orange ski jacket, with all of its holes, can still keep me warm.

I may sound optimistic, but it's just a survival mechanism.

My shitty Walkman is the most reliable thing I have. It's chewed all but one of my tapes, but they weren't that good to begin with. On humid days, my winter itch goes away, but the Walkman goes wonky and I have to hold it upside-down to play Duran Duran properly because of a battery connection that operates on gravity.

Everything has a survival mechanism.

It's amazing how something so fragile never lets me down, even when it's raining acid from New Jersey, when the cheap batteries I stole from the discount pharmacy are almost dead, and when I'm running out of ideas how to stay alive.

I might have crabs and my lip ring might be crusting again.

Whatever.

I might have athlete's foot from squatting in wet sneakers, and the pharmacy might be closed so I can't lift a tube of Polysporin and whatever else I need to fix my shit.

Shopping problems, those I can deal with.

There might even be a tapeworm gnawing a hole through my stomach out of secondary hunger, but if I hold my Walkman just right, the music plays and the world is perfect.

And when the outside world gets too oppressive, I can always go home.

There are only two things that can ruin my day.

The first is when my pen explodes during a really heavy piece of fiction. Not heavy in the sense that it *makes* the ink explode, but in the sense that the interruption is annoying. I get covered in ink more often than you'd believe. I use Bic medium black exclusively, though it's not because I'm a brand hound. Bics happen to be the most reliable pens on the market, and the hexagonal shape is perfect for rewinding tapes when your batteries are fizzling out.

I've used a fancy Montblanc before, and trust me, they're shit. With all the research they put into it, you'd think the ballpoint wouldn't gum up so often. There are two ways to unstick a pen—either doodle while pressing like your wrist is going to snap, or char the tip with a lighter. Both ways, there's a sixty-forty chance you're getting an ink shower.

To answer your question, I've tried Papermate pens, but their medium is so thick, it's like writing with a marker—you can't be subtle. And besides, they explode too often.

The other thing that can sour a perfect day is when someone strays into my home, my modest but well-appointed apartment, and interrupts my writing by asking me if I work there. I have to hold myself back from sticking a high heel in their neck, and then I put on my best customer service smile.

I want you to picture the kind of customer I'm talking about. She's wearing a pair of charcoal pants with bias-cut hems and razor pleats and a translucent chiffon top with batwing sleeves. The tulle chinoiserie is just to rub your face in it. If you're wondering how I know this terminology, it's because I've served enough of these idiots to know how they describe themselves. They do it quite often. This woman, she wears perfume from concentrate, and applies lipstick thinking that her mouth spans more face than it actually does. This is a Fiorucci woman. The Fiorucci woman's biggest problem has always been finding the right shoes, the ones she needs to crush people like me beneath her.

I am here to help.

"Of course I work here."

"Do you have a size seven stiletto in sea foam green?"

"Close your eyes."

"Can't you just answer my question?"

"This is part of the Fiorucci experience," I say. "Now close your eyes and imagine waves crashing on the shore, pushing sea foam up the beach ... What color is it?"

"The water?"

"The foam."

This is usually the part when I start winning the conversation.

"Umm ... it's kind of whitish."

"So shouldn't it be sea foam white?"

"My Visa limit is probably twice your annual salary, you little shit ... I don't deserve this. Where's the manager?"

"I can call her, but you still won't be able to get those goat hooves into a size seven."

That's usually when they storm out, realizing I don't work there, and that they've accidentally discovered a stock-room stowaway. Then I hide in the only place no one will check, in a crate of fall/winter 1998—no one wants to be seen rooting through last season's rejects, no one with Fiorucci in the blood. I camp out until things settle down and home becomes a tranquil place again, a place without customers.

Sometimes it's hard getting back home, especially after closing time. They keep changing the alarm code on me, and then I'm locked out until I spy on someone punching it in. When I spray-paint the motion sensor, they buy a new one, and when I bust the back door so the latch doesn't lock, it's so fudged up that I can't get in. On busy days, I can take a shoe order, walk right back there and never come out, kind of like how I discovered the stock room in the first place.

You're probably wondering why I can't get a real home, even with all the whore money I make. I can't understand it either. I'm staring at a crisp, hundred-dollar bill that's utterly useless.

Motel rooms, the scuzzy ones with bedbugs, start at seventy-five, but I can't afford the security deposit. They want me to pay for all the damage I might do, when the worst would be writing story notes on the bathroom wall while taking a shit.

Fold in half, right along Ben Franklin's nose.

Apartment landlords want three months up front, and family references.

Fold both sides kitty-corner into the middle.

Hostels won't let me in because they're suspicious of that new shoe smell I walk around with and can't wash off.

Bend back the wings.

And nevermind bribing doormen to sleep in building basements. Thing is, tenants tip them enough at Christmas to make sure that designer riff-raff like me can't use their zip code.

Crease little triangles at the tips.

Some places are free, like shelters, but show me one that's cleaner than a stock room. Show me one where I can lay my head on purses of soft Italian leather. Show me one where I can walk barefoot on double-weave cotton suits with gold threading. Show me one where I can eat cereal out of a different high heel every day.

Tear a strip at the back for flight control.

Release.

One day, I might move to a city where hundred-dollar bills are more than just paper airplanes.

It's New Year's Eve, minutes away from spilling into 1999. All the screams and body-fucking. There's nothing I can do but squeeze closer to whatever's at the middle of this commotion.

Worm my way through the crowd that's distending Times Square twenty extra blocks. Blinking lights. Noise and hum stretching the top of my mind up, up, up. Starspin until I'm dizzy and deaf. This thrumming has no beginning or end, and will be here long after I'm gone.

Erase. Clear history. I could be deleted data, I could be stardust, and I could be nowhere in particular.

Some people have kids. Some people leave bullets inside other people. Some people tell jokes that get told and told. The point is that everyone leaves something, a little trace of themselves, behind.

I have writing. It's the proof I can give that there was something worth doing. You know what I mean. That not everything was for nothing. I know you're wondering what I'm so compelled to write about, but you'll eventually find out. Just to forewarn you, I write about things I find, so it's not always pretty or poetic.

The millennium's here. People are saying that it's all going to break apart. Even atheists admit that there's some kind of reckoning coming.

So I think it would be good to get something published. As a matter of fact, I'm going to give myself until the end of 1999 to make it as a writer. And if that doesn't happen, I will very methodically kill the dream in front of your eyes, in such a graphic way that you will never believe in dreams again. Not because I'm mean, but because you shouldn't believe in things that are supposed to come true, but don't.

When I write at night, I turn into a superhero. There are superheroes all over the city, and they need darkness to hide how normal they really are.

Sometimes I abuse my powers. I steal the first newspaper delivered in the city, from the steps of City Hall at four a.m.

Mayor Giuliani can suck my wang.

Kurt Vonnegut has always tweaked it for me, so when he came to speak at the Barnes and Noble bookstore in Union Square, I didn't mind skipping out on a well-paying trick.

K.V.'s written all of my favorite novels, the ones I can handle because he wrote them in snippets.

His lectures were famous for magic tricks—bunny rabbits, hidden bouquets—yet that wasn't why I went.

I don't know what I was expecting. Maybe I thought he would grab my notebook, read a few paragraphs to the crowd, and toast me as the next writing sensation. Maybe I thought his greatness would rub off on me, polish me around the edges.

A security guard filled the door frame just as I was about to walk in. He was wearing crappy loafers that looked like they were from Kmart, and I could see where the sole glue was coming undone.

"Sir, the bookstore is full. We cannot accommodate any more guests for Mr Vonnegut's appearance."

From outside, I could see all kinds of room between bookshelves and behind display tables.

"I don't mind listening from the second floor. It doesn't matter where I am."

"Then you won't mind listening from outside."

I tried to squeeze past him but he pinned me against the molding and pushed me back outside. His radio crackled.

"It's nothing personal, but we can't let you in. I said we're full."

I sniffed the armpits of my ski jacket to see if it was street stink that had turned him off or the smell of designer leather and treated snakeskin. Nothing. Smelled like winter. He started to close the door. I jammed my foot in the crack and he kicked it out.

"It's nothing personal."

Of course it wasn't. He was just doing his job, making sure I understood that my place was on the outside of the glass, fogging it up.

My nostrils misted the window until I couldn't see anything. I had to imagine K.V.'s magic tricks, imagine them from scratch.

Not that I'd gone there for the tricks.

Why New York City is not America:

Because not everyone has a gun or thinks they need one, because the industrial smog that wafts over from New Jersey creates a sunset I want to lick off the sky, because people live in the subway, because some of the homeless live better than housed people in other cities.

Because people don't wish you "God bless," because God would feel uncomfortable among the godless skyscrapers of Manhattan, because an old woman can keep her rent-controlled apartment for twenty-six dollars a month.

Because there are four daily papers that can spin a story four different ways, dividing the city into quadrants of people who can't, for obvious reasons, chat about the news.

Because people die when the power goes out.

I don't want to talk about how I got my eye busted open, because looking back is dangerous. You have to keep moving forward to stave off death. Thank God I'm not homeless, because I'd really be fucked if I didn't have a place to crash and recuperate between wounds.

Right about the time that I was debating whether or not to let the winter wind freeze-clot the blood, or maybe tamp it with some relatively unused Ray's Pizza napkins, somebody walked into my blur.

"Hey there."

"What do you want."

Sometimes when I ask a question, it doesn't sound like one.

"Nothing. Listen, why don't you let me take care of that eye for you. It could get infected if you don't do it right."

He was a blond guy, twenty-seven or twenty-eight and kind of preppy-looking. He was holding a bunch of flowers, and not the cheap ones, either. He was cute enough for me to forgive his inferior Pumas. It's not that Fiorucci has warped my outlook on the world or turned me into a snob, but you'll destroy your insteps if you wear anything else.

"Okay."

"Cool."

"Yes, it is."

We smiled at each other. It had been a while since anyone had shown me their teeth in a nonaggressive manner.

I walked home with him, and he carried my duffel bag. I turned off my pager so we could be alone.

Derek was scrubbing Coast soap into a hand-puppet washcloth. I was slumped naked on the shower floor, twirling my pubic hair, watching the brown water swirl down the drain.

"How's it going there?"

"Whatever," I said.

He started by washing my chest, then my back, then behind my ears, doting over me like I was going to melt away. I noticed a certain softness to Derek that afternoon, even though I was sure, at the time, that he was just a pervert with a knack for psychology. His head was getting soaked in the shower stream, and the tips of his matted bangs tickled my neck and gave me goose bumps.

"Outside," he said. "Why did you ask me if I wanted anything?"

"You clearly have no concept of how the world works. It doesn't surprise me."

"What is that supposed to mean?"

"Well, don't take this the wrong way, but ... it's obvious that money's kind of ruined it for you."

"You're a rude little snot, aren't you?" he said.

I watched the blood dribble down my body and pool between my legs, circling around the drain like little red spider webs.

"Did you call the police?" he asked.

"Huh?"

"For what they did to you."

"As an independent businessperson, I'd rather bleed here than in jail."

"Your eye doesn't look very good. I mean, it looks great but it probably hurts."

"Maybe you can do something with it."

He grazed the skin just below the cut, pressing ever so gently with the tip of the washcloth, opening the wound to the water.

"Ow."

"It's turning the most incredible color," Derek said. "Like a ... like a pomegranate dropped from a window. Two days in the sun. Three."

Somehow I knew that he was fascinated by all kinds of gruesome stuff. I thought about showing him the toe funk I'd been farming through the winter.

He turned off the water.

"Dark towel, please, so ..."

"I know," Derek said.

I was pissed at myself. I hadn't shown him yet, but I had fallen for tenderness, a trap that has worked on stupid, trusting animals ever since they were first fucked into the world.

"I'd like to paint now," he said. "I'm thinking ... something the color of your eye."

Because you can buy beer at five a.m. from a pharmacy, because you can get Montreal bagels with cream cheese in ice cream flavors like pistachio and Cherry Garcia, because everyone is an actor and no one is a waiter, because everyone "does" something and it's usually something other than what they actually do, because area codes determine your place in the food chain, because you are always in the food chain and you can never, ever take a break.

Even without the telescope of time to back us up, we both knew it was the beginning. The beginning of a relationship that neither of us might ever understand, nor be able to criticize, nor be able to live with, nor be able to undo.

Derek Brathwaite was arranging flowers in a vase on a painter's table in the middle of the loft. His wet blond bangs kept nudging the bouquet out of whack, so he had to do it a few times. I liked watching him lose his mind like that. There were only two tulips and a swollen lilac head.

I was drinking coffee by the big square windowpanes—typical of Chelsea's converted factories, I'm told—letting the afternoon sun dry my naked body. I wasn't used to the heat, and couldn't keep his bathrobe on.

I was both impressed and confused by the size of the loft—the distance between piles of clutter was hard to measure. Past a heap of canvases were towers of art magazines with names like *S.P.A.C.E.* and *New Paradigm*, teetering over an even scatter of paint tubes on the floor. There were stacks of photos everywhere, shots of boys in trouble piled waist-high, and there was a stripped-down jet engine near the door, maybe a replica, maybe a crash-site score.

The kitchen was a corner of the loft where I learned the extent of Derek's problem. Water ionizer, blender, food processor, KitchenAid tilt-head stand mixer, juicer, vacuum sealer, Wolfgang Puck Electric SwivelBaker (for waffles), Mikasa hand-cut lead crystal stemware, Wedgwood fine bone china by Vera Wang, Hamilton Beach BrewStation Deluxe, and casual place settings for eight, broken and reglued for style.

It really bothered me that he was missing a toaster.

On the floor, in the middle of it all, was a rectangular frame made of two-by-four wood planks, fencing in two turtles.

"I thought you were going to paint something," I said.

Derek carefully lifted up one turtle at a time, sliding a sheet of canvas under them in the box. He kissed their shells.

"I lost the impulse. The problem was that we cleaned your eye too quickly. The lighting in the bathroom was bad."

"I don't understand."

He wandered over to a pile of Polaroids, rooted through them, then emerged with an armful and handed them to me.

"Take a look at these."

Grainy shots of crying boys with knee scrapes full of gravel. Dubious medical procedures, strange tools. Faces squinched in pain. Teen hoodlums slammed against cars, wrists cuffed tight, shocked faces reflected in the hood shine. Gloomy and insolent. Bloody noses that puberty had already made too conspicuous. The world ending before they turned sixteen.

I was almost expecting to find a picture of myself.

"Who are they," I said.

"Concentrated inspiration. Useless boys."

Derek strapped Magic Markers on the turtles' backs with rubber bands, the thick blue ones you find holding broccoli spears together at the supermarket.

"I haven't been able to paint for two dry, damn years. The pictures don't do it for me anymore because I can't trick myself into believing that those bruises are fresh. Pretty boys heal quickly. You know."

The walls of the loft were lined with canvases, warm jumbles of squiggly lines and Day-Glo colors that had little to do with Derek.

He snapped the rubber bands and the scaly turtle legs revved into gear. They set off on separate adventures, to different corners of the two-by-four box, tracing their jerky paths behind them in fluorescent purple and orange.

"There are three rules," Derek said gravely, taking the photos out of my hands. "Rent is three hundred dollars a month."

"Shouldn't you be paying me?"

"What for?"

I stared at the king-sized mattress in the middle of the loft, the only bed in sight.

"To be determined."

"I think I had something else in mind."

"This place has to be a few grand. Why don't you charge me thirteen hundred, I'll charge you a thousand, and you'll get your three hundred dollars."

"What's the difference?"

"If we're not going to have receipts and invoices, then we at least need pretend ones, to know where we stand."

"You've done this before," he said.

"Yeah, but at least the guy had a toaster. Or I'll charge you back thirteen hundred and I'll get you a pair of Fioruccis."

"Huh?"

I pointed to his Pumas.

"Your insteps."

"I have an idea, weirdo," he said, showing me the demonic gleam I'd come to know. "Since you want to play house, I'll raise the rent to two thousand and pretend to love you."

"That wasn't nice," I said. "Do you even need my money?"

"Listen, you're the one who wants to be official about this."

"About what?"

"God, you're complicated. Rule number two. If you end up leaving, don't steal anything from me."

"I reserve the right to take back the fucking shoes."

"And three, you must never, ever take care of a wound yourself unless you're farther than a cab ride from home."

This looked like it was going to work out just fine.

Some days, there's nothing to do but smoke. Those are usually the days it's too cold to hold anything in your fingers.

I notice things. The entire city of New York smells like garbage and flowers. You can buy daisies in winter, dyed Kool-Aid colors and frost-proofed with shellac. Rats arrange bouquets out of the junk people throw out:

Broken high heels, alligator-skin pumps dyed the wrong robin's egg blue, clogs that stink of champagne, wingtip bucks missing Swarovski crystals, vinyl vamps peeling off, open-toe stilettos covered in mascara, silver sandals covered in mud, slip-ons with the tassels snipped off.

Some of the stuff I notice is so fascinating, I do a little collecting, too.

Wink and Nod, having eaten a fortune in greenhouse produce (a.k.a. turtle fuel), started to mill restlessly around their box. Nod liked her shell to be tapped so I drummed out a remix of "Tainted Love." Derek was busy in the kitchen making us fusilli pasta and artichoke hearts with a goat cheese Alfredo sauce.

"Jaeven, can you strap on the Magic Markers? Let's get a masterpiece going before they shit out too much creative energy."

"What colors?"

"Blue and green. They look kind of surfish and oceanic today."

"You're the genius."

I uncapped the markers and strapped them on the turtles. I'm firmly convinced that each of us has a rubber band around us that can snap at anytime. We either have to be ready for it, or cut ourselves loose before it happens.

He wasn't kidding about being oceanic. Today, the turtles were drawing a great big rollicking sea smacking of salt and adventure. They were marching around, bumping tock-tock-tock into the two-by-fours of their rectangular world, their microcosm, what Derek had dubbed TraceBox™.

Sometimes they will draw at night. We'll be lying in bed and I'll listen to their headlong plods, the persistent knocks into deterrents that don't work, wondering if they're as incapable of feeling (or as capable of unfeeling) as people can be. On their bad days they act like us, turning in circles around and around, leaving pathetic scratchings in corners of the canvas, markings accumulated monotonously on top of each other.

The lines can be bold and straight, like the ones explorers etch into the earth. Other times they're nervous and uncertain. There are even trails that begin, disappear, and resume elsewhere, as if Wink and Nod fly to whatever parts of the canvas they deem worthy of their art-making.

"Who buys these?" I asked him. "Fans of Teenage Mutant—"

I shut up because he stopped dismantling the artichoke in his hands and gave me a searing look.

"Collectors who want to throw the most postmodern parties. Postcolonialists who find it funny when artists employ animals to do their intellectual dirty work for them."

"I see," I said.

"I don't give a crap who buys them," Derek continued, "just as long as they pay. But I'm tired of being recognized for my pets. I used to be better than them, you know."

"Are you talking about the paintings in the storage closet?"

"How did you get in there? Listen, I don't want you poking around through my life failures like that."

"Sorry, but I was curious why you have all these paint supplies lying around if you don't paint anymore."

"Good question," he said angrily.

"Derek, I didn't mean it that way," I said.

The dinner was tinged that night. It was bitter and over-cooked, some flavors a little frustrated. We swallowed too loudly.

That night, we crawled into our princess-and-the-pea bed in the middle of the loft and listened to the sound of shells knocking on wood.

When that stopped, we listened to each other's breathing, and to the silence between us.

I have a place to live, a great guy to cook and care for me, and an address where I can receive mail from publishers.

Derek has a muse who hasn't inspired him yet.

Life could always be more, well, fair.

I don't write poetry, but if I did, this is what it might look like:

Flowers withering in the dark, cutting your leg with a razor blade when you feel sad, private performances nobody attends, snakes molting, deer shedding antlers in the woods, seahorses hooking tails.

When Derek handed the envelope to me, I had to read my name a few times before I could believe that the US Postal Service considered me a person. It was from *Circle* magazine, a literary journal I had sent a short story to.

The story.

A kid was reading Dostoevsky's *Crime and Punishment* in English Lit, mouthing the words silently to himself in class, wondering if he was reading in Russian or in English. He couldn't tell, but it didn't matter. (I had this writing book called *Avoiding the Draft*. Good writers, page eighty-four says, foreshadow story elements like retreating soldiers plant landmines.)

The teacher asked him to read a passage out loud. The kid started off reading as it was written, word for word, but then five pages into it, veered off the page and into text nobody else could see. There was laughter. Confusion. Fury. (Good writers, page ninety-nine says, take readers through an emotional battlefield.)

The kid was channeling drafts that Dostoevsky had trashed when he was slogging through the manuscript more than a century ago in Russia. The kid was rescuing the crumpled sheets from Fyodor's wooden wastepaper basket, or papier-mâché bin, or whatever they used for receptacles back then.

Someone screamed genius. Someone else screamed ADD. The kid calmly informed them that it was neither, that it was a gift from above, and that they had better shut up so he wouldn't lose any of the text.

The school called his parents who called the doctors who medicated him. Pumped him full of Ritalin. As his final literature project that year, he turned in a newly revised 1865 draft of *Crime and Punishment*, casting himself as the tortured Raskolnikov, whom the world was out to get.

Judging from the amount of work I put into the story, the number of times I rewrote it, and my constant trips into Strunk and White's *Elements of Style*, I thought it was pretty good. The story was circular, and I thought that a magazine called *Circle* would, at the very least, be able to pick up on that.

Here's the response I got:

Dear Mr Marshall,

Thank you for sending us your short story, "An Improbable Gift." We have chosen not to send an impersonal rejection slip, because we feel the need to point out how particularly inappropriate this submission is for our magazine.

It is amazing how many writers fail to read the submission guidelines.

We do not publish first drafts.

We do not publish teenage revenge fantasies.

We do not publish stories that contain more than one instance of the word "overwrought." This is specifically mentioned in the submission guidelines.

We do not publish stories that are not fully thought out. What is your character's connection to nineteenth-century Russia? In other words, why Dostoevsky? And if his gift is supposed to be from God (because we can't perceive any other source), don't you think that God would direct the character to a less atheistic writer?

Thank you for submitting to Circle, and please read an issue before the next time you do so.

The Publishers

I followed their advice today and stole all the copies of Circle I could find in Manhattan. I went to uptown magazine stores, to the Gem Spa newsstand in the East Village, and scoured Chelsea clean.

Good writers are determined writers, page twelve says, and determined writers don't take bullets lying down.

So I went to Chelsea Piers on the Hudson River, laid the magazines in a perfect circle, screamed the word "overwrought" to a passing barge, and lit a fucking match.

Because AIDS and HIV aren't ignored as much, because people read books, because everybody's from Canada or Puerto Rico, because nothing west of the Hudson River matters or even exists, because you can throw away a magazine and magically buy the same one ten minutes later from a recycling technician.

Because a young man is doomed to live in a Fiorucci store if he doesn't want to whore himself out in some degrading office job.

Because writers can make it here no matter what.

Today, a jerk-wad stuffed a hundred between my cheeks, poking it in that extra half-inch with his pinky, so it would be tainted with the stink of my ass. That Franklin is forever connected, as long as its circulation life will last, with the ass that earned it this afternoon.

But he didn't end it there. He donkey-punched me in the ribs and left me gasping behind the garbage container. I followed Derek's orders and limped, screaming and bent over sideways, into a taxi. The driver said he didn't change hundreds so I cursed him in a rather racist way and found one who'd take it.

Derek spent the better part of an hour tending to my ribs, watching the bruises shift floridly through the color spectrum. I was splayed on his lap, arched over his knees staring at the ceiling, the skin stretched tight over my ribs. He was watching me breathe, scribbling notes.

Ninety-two dollars and thirteen cents, after cab fare. That means I'll have to go through this hell at least two more times before rent is due, maybe three.

Now that I think about it, I might not give Derek those shoes after all.

It's best to hurt yourself before anyone else can do it for you. At least you know how deep the cut or how purple the bruise will be.

Fuck-you notes in champagne bottles cast to sea, private blackness left to ache to itself, a lifetime of secrets and a headful of inside jokes, breakup emails snagged by the spam filter.

Derek was busy blowing his head open with color experiments.

I learned to recognize the pattern: a crazy look in his eye, shades of an impossible hue splashing itself on the inside of his head, and then days of pouring and mixing, tinting and distilling, all in a mad quest to replicate it in reality so his world could be sane. Anyone in his position would do the same. The rainbows you see have to match the ones in your head. They just have to.

Say it's a shade of Ajax blue that haunts him, some shadowy mix of peacock and ultramarine, with a touch of afternoon sky. There's a certain Sunlight dish-soap yellow that's elusive and hard to describe, even though there's no mistaking it. Or it will be the ice-mint green in his tube of Aquafresh.

I remind him that not every color in the household product universe is sold in tubes, or can be replicated, but he disagrees. He won't give up.

He'll agonize over a seafood cream sauce for hours, hunched over a nonstick T-Fal pan brooding over the tint, wondering if white was always off-white, becoming more sure with every stir that only the blind can see the color that milk is supposed to be.

Here is a partial list of the color schemes that Derek spends his life trying to create, with varying degrees of success:

Nasturtiums bashed to death in their own pollen.

Butterfly wings lit by moonlight.

Tire skid marks on new pavement.

Charred African violets dipped in wine.

Brittle hail in a lightning storm.

Cut-up gums medicated with strawberry juice.

Sea foam green.

The scabby red of scratch marks healing on my back.

The blackening of blood is particularly hard to capture because it's always in a state of change. Derek can never decide when it's reached the peak of beauty. He fawns over my back from moment to moment.

He dribbles and spatters, stirs and folds, mashes and kaleidoscopes until the insanity of being perpetually *almost there* makes him throw the whole mess against the wall.

And, of course, colors are never the same when they dry.

I have something to confess to you. That part about getting beat up behind a dumpster, it wasn't all true. I'm kind of embarrassed about it, but I wanted you to experience the emotional grit I felt. The guy was real, and so was the hundred bucks between my cheeks, but he fucked me in a hotel room, not behind a dumpster. It's just that I wanted you to see me the same way he did—as a piece of trash. If I told you about the room service and champagne bucket, would you have been able to relate to my pain? Probably not.

The donkey-punch was also a bit of a stretch. It was more of a play-ful slap, but I needed you to see the humiliation in full bleeding color. The bruises were real, but I had to give them to myself. I had to make the outside of me match the inside of me.

I know what you're thinking. You're wondering if everything I've told you is a lie, and you have every right to be suspicious. But you have to know that I'll never lie outright, I'll just transform, until you get the point of what I'm trying to say.

I haven't had a friend in years. Derek doesn't count because our web gets sticky. I'm talking about someone you can spill your guts to without worrying you'll hurt them. Emotions on a dimmer switch.

You know ... a buddy?

Cops on every corner, undercover feds in navy blue Crown Victorias, detectives pretending to be cab drivers.

Multiplying like amoebae, ticketing urinators, narcing through the five boroughs, talking sideways into radios, cleaning up, ticketing smokers, bleaching Broadway, closing peep shows, clamping down, speeding up, erasing the smell of cum from Eighth Avenue, the smell of beer from the subway, ticketing other cops, hauling in rent boys, stealing joints, stealing turf, turning shoplifting into a bloodsport, catching us all.

I'm beginning to wonder if I'll ever get published. They say that writers should scribble something every day, but these days the words come so hard.

I can't even write at alt.coffee, a supposed writers' café where inspiration comes in three forms: iced coffees, lattes, and Nanaimo bars with some kind of insane shit in them, either speed or Drano.

The incessant whine of the coffee grinder isn't what bothers me, and it's not the horrible décor: decrepit sofas in puke yellow and blister red, lamps with torn velvet shades. It's not even the conspiracy nuts, swapping theories over deafening laptop key clatter, who drive me crazy. They talk about the Internet as if it'll still be around in five years.

It's the actors, the ones so slick that gum doesn't even stick to their shoes, who make me want to retch.

A Colgate smile flashed in front of my face.

"Hey, I'm Chase, and a school bus crushed my legs."

They looked intact to me.

"*Terror Firmer* by Troma Films."

"Excuse me?"

"He's an actor and he's almost famous," an earthy girl beside him said. "Famous people are allowed to speak in incomplete sentences. I'm Forest."

"Oh."

"They had a school bus crush my legs."

"Brilliant," I said.

"He is," Forest said from under her beige Stevie Nicks shawl.

"Are you famous, too?" I said.

She smiled like she had eaten a lemon.

"So what do you do, dude?" Chase asked me.

That shock of conditioner-soaked hair.

"I enjoy life."

He and Forest laughed in measured staccato notes like they had rehearsed this before. I was playing my part exceptionally well, considering this was my first run-through.

"You have to do *something*," she said. "You can't *not* do anything. This is *New York*."

"I'm a writer."

"Rock the Casbah," Chase said.

"Wait—are you published?" Forest said.

"Not yet."

"So then what do you really do? Don't be ashamed of how you spend your life."

"Dude, he said that he's a writer. He's cool."

Chase checked out the café, I'm guessing to see who was admiring his hair, and Forest took my hand in hers in a creepy way.

"I can feel that you're a communicator." Her eyes shot wide open.

"A *great* one. Unpublished writers have so much potential. You're bursting, aren't you? I can ... mmm ... feel it."

"I *told* you he was a writer," Chase said, and slapped me on the back.

I know I'm going to sound like a snob, but it needs to be said—if you don't have Fiorucci sneakers like mine, your life will be shit, and I can prove it.

Do you think blisters are the way to happiness? If you're not wearing calfskin uppers, you're going to need a lifetime supply of Band-Aids. Hacks like Salvatore Ferragamo think they can get away with rubber soles when they should be leather, while cheapskates like Bruno Magli use proper leather soles but make them too thin. They either want you to destroy your arches or puncture yourself with city sharps.

I wonder how Manolo Blahnik expects to build a fashion brand around glue. Even people who cripple themselves with mediocre footwear know that sewn construction is the only way to keep a shoe together. It's common sense.

I should work the clubs, Derek told me, if I wanted to get a less violent clientele. That was nice of him. He went so far as to suggest the club, this Derek. This uninspired painter who needed my bruises.

It's an unseasonably hot winter night. March came early this year— a spring hijacking.

Stinking, rotting meat. Lamb's blood putrefying on the sidewalk, and it isn't even Passover. Entrails that lazy meat handlers couldn't be bothered to pick up. Chicken gizzards, or giblets, or whatever the hell they're called. The snow has melted and mixed with the blood, and this pinkish liquid is running over the curb.

I love the Meatpacking District.

It's a Disneyland of death, shoe stores, and clubs. I pass The Lure, a club that I heard still has the original meat-hooks. You can hang your coat on them, car keys, balls, whatever. It's a slightly more upscale sex pit than The Manhole, which is just a few blocks over on Tranny Way. Ninth Avenue, I mean.

Sneakerful of meat juice.

Joe's Steakhouse, Lambs Unlimited, Prada. A perfect trinity on every block. If I told you the name "Hogs and Heifers," I bet you couldn't guess what they do.

I soccer-kick a sheep's eyeball into the sewer.

I find it no coincidence that the first night I walk through New York feeling reasonably empowered is the same night the streets are washed slick with animal blood, warm and feverish.

Things are looking up for me. I've managed to start a new story that I can't talk about yet because it might interfere with the creative process, but I can tell you that it's freaking intestinal. And I've found someone. Derek is stabilizing my life, though I don't trust our relationship completely yet. It's too perfect. It's hard to let go of a history of failure that likes to repeat itself.

Jackie 60 is the club that nobody knows about but everybody goes to.

I walk in wearing a T-shirt I bummed from Derek that says "Rape the Twinks." The Columbia art school hipsters are giving me dirty looks for being more ironic than they are.

The upstairs bores me immediately. It's this over-glamorized holding room lined with faux Louis XIV divans and aging queers holding martinis. Blah. They rot while Blondie videos run on a constant loop.

In the basement, I descend into the pure thump of Eurythmics, courtesy of DJ Johnny Dynell.

The eighties are the new nineties, they say.

The drunken dancers know it and they're doing the barley mash. There are the usual hardened lumps of sex and other reminders that we're young and free and we own the universe (well, most of us).

I order a vodka cranberry, I don't pay for it, and I don't ask questions.

There seems to be some confusion that I'm a dancer and not doing my job, and the crowd kind of pushes me onstage with collective indignation.

Shit. I'm thrust into this BDSM church scene, turns out I'm an altar boy fucking a priest while a nun hung on a giant fiberglass cross is whipping her clit. I don't know how I inhabited this role so easily—it's like I've been fucking priests all my life.

Now I'm making a mess because I'm rocking Father doggy-style while spilling a Long Island Iced Tea that somehow replaced my vodka cranberry.

The song ends, the nun cums on her rosary, and somebody unhooks her from the cross. The priest falls face down and about twenty guys stick singles in my waistband. Some of them fondle my bulge. What the fuck. Then one guy slips me a twenty and buries his face in my jeans. The others get their cue to scatter.

"Care for a drink?"

His politesse sounds fake because he's gawking at me from the inside of a beer glass. I don't officially work here, so I can "turn down business" without getting thrown out by the tranny bouncers, but something about the idea of taking advantage of this jerk appeals to me.

I own this city. I can feel it somewhere deep in my gut, that feeling of ownership that comes with being the master of desire for so many rich, pathetic, whinging American men.

Historically, they've been the ones in charge, but little revolutions happen every day.

It's time to take control.

It's time my freaking balls dropped.

But I'm not really paying attention to him anymore. There's a goth boy staring at me from across the dance floor. He's darkly beautiful. Twenty, twenty-one. A heavy Neanderthal brow inched over long, wet lashes. Eyes that are impervious to the strobe lights, where thoughts pool, drain, and refill. His gelled hair is bed-sexy—every spike is exactly where it shouldn't be.

I like the message he's sending me.

"I said, care for a drink?"

I'm spacing out, and surprised to see that my trick's still there. I finally get a good look at him. He's pretty cute, with just enough hair to still be sexy for a thirty-something, but I'm not going to let him get me that easily.

"No thanks, I'm still working on my iced tea."

"You have a great ass. Mind if I touch it?"

"You can't afford it."

I jump off the stage. The other clubbers have cleared a space around us.

"Here's a hundred bucks," he says.

"What the fuck for?"

"For nothing ... For being sexy. Well, actually, if I'm giving you a hundred, I want you to use my name. It's Jason."

"Hi Paul."

Tricks like it when you fuck with them like that. I give him my tough punk look, my raised eyebrow and lip sneer, and take the money.

"It's only half of the two hundred I won in a bet that I couldn't get you off the stage. I don't mind losing it."

I was obviously dealing with a professional. But a professional what?

Paul points to his friends drooling at the bar. They're getting me more drinks, I can tell by the parade of rainbow-colored cocktail umbrellas.

I'm getting woozy. I hold my glass up to the strobe lights and swish it around. It splashes in arrested clicks of time, but I can't see anything suspicious dissolving on the bottom.

"I might be able to give you the other hundred," he says, chewing his liquor. "What do you do?"

That question.

"I'm a writer."

"Perrrfect. I happen to be doing a photographic project on New York writers in the nude."

I love seeing the flicker of a lie in a trick's eyes. It makes me pre-cum.

We leave Jackie 60, I sit my ass down in the taxi, and we're off.

Stuff I just happen to come across:

Snot wads frozen into gumdrops on the sidewalk in winter, rats speared by syringes, Lego revolvers, hair-weave tumbleweed, congealed balls of motor oil, barely recognizable people lost in building cracks, doggie mud pies you find by surprise when the snow melts, ants swarming popsicle sticks in summer.

While we crossed the bridge to Williamsburg, an industrial-cum-hipster Brooklyn neighborhood, I sat alone in the back seat of the cab, chauffeured. Paul told me that it was good we were both artists because artists could feed off each other.

Did he honestly think I was falling for his crap?

The elevator doors opened to his loft and he flipped a set of switches. On came the lights and The Verve's "Bittersweet Symphony," and the blinds retracted to give a twinkling view of the Manhattan skyline.

Living pretty large for an artist, he was.

"Get comfortable."

I pulled my notebook out of my back pocket and laid it on the giant Lego coffee table, then flopped into a La-Z-Boy chair and put my feet up.

"I mean take off your clothes."

"How much are you paying me?"

"Two hundred. These shots might not even get printed. I'm only doing it to keep my camera from rusting."

"Three hundred or I walk."

"Have fun walking over the bridge. Two hundred."

"And fifty."

"Two hundred. If I give you an extra fifty, it'll be a tip because I like you."

I wasn't sure if I was going to be able to take control, so far from the street, so far from my comfort zone. He loaded film into his camera and tossed the empty plastic canister like a peanut shell. I shucked my jeans.

"Tell me about your writing."

"It would go over your head."

"I like it when you're saucy. Give your cock a squeeze. Make it purple and angry for me ... Riiiiiiight."

Click, flash, and that electronic camera whirrrr.

"Now give me a sad face ... Sadder. Think about your mother dying. Your cat chasing a moth into the fireplace. Photography is about emotion. Good."

I followed his orders even though I knew he was full of shit, only because I wanted to be professional.

"You know," he said, "I'm friends with a few publishers. Stretch your foreskin out and show me some pit."

I got a full boner just hearing that magic word. The "P" word. I cranked an elbow behind my head and leaned back in the La-Z-Boy. He shot the worshipper's view from the floor, angling the camera squarely at my crotch. Click, whirrrr. Some shots of my chicken-white thighs with their goosebumps, then my balls, and up my shaft, inch by inch.

This camera lens climbing my genitalia left me feeling strangely powerful. My wang throbbed to the smell in my nose, the smell of the ink of my future books.

"They say that the best manuscripts are illegible. Coffee, ink, blood stains. They call the writer in to decipher, to read in his own voice.

It kills them. Publishing contract with a big advance. I'm excited for you."

Snap, click, whirrrr. He was giving me funny looks.

"We're almost done. I want to get some relaxed shots of you drinking whisky. All the famous writers knew how to appreciate a good rye blend. You can even write if you like."

He poured me a highball the color of diluted apple juice. I had no reason to suspect him. If he'd really wanted to, he could've slipped me a roofie at the club, and right now he and his barfly friends would be nailing me shitless.

"Take a sip."

Click, whirrrr.

"Again."

Snap.

"Fantastic. Now, one last shot. Flop your dick in the glass like the whole world's turning upside-down and it doesn't matter what you do."

I did it and was suddenly lightheaded. Everything felt perfect and dreamy in a way I didn't trust, like something was wrong, but in such a remote way that it was beyond the reach of my brain. It was kind of David Lynch.

"That's it," he said.

"What do you mean."

"You can go home now."

He hadn't even asked for a cumshot, or tried to jerk me off or finger my asshole. What the fuck. And he paid me two hundred bucks, on top of the hundred he'd given me at Jackie 60.

On the elevator down, there was that otherworldly lightness again.

I suppose it matters less how you fall asleep on the train than where you end up.

The city was bass-ackwards when I woke up in Brooklyn. It was morning. I must've gotten my nod on, sleepwalked a switch from the L train to the D, and ran the forty-one station line a couple of times, end to end.

The white sand on the elevated subway platform crunched under my shoes. The sun swelled my hangover to a full skull ache, and the salt in the air made me lick my lips. I gazed out at a body of water that didn't end, just got hazier. Below, the waves were rumbling like blue Pontiacs over the beach, a beach that stretched your eyes for miles in both directions, past the rusty metal skeletons of amusement park rides under lockdown.

If there was an ocean in Brooklyn, wouldn't someone have tipped me off?

I wasn't going to spend time making sense of Coney Island that day, not before I had slept properly or had at least gotten a cup of coffee. I turned to wait for the D train to take me back to Manhattan, but since it was the end of the line, the train was still there and the doors were still open.

Initials carved into a tree scheduled to be chopped down, lucky pennies dropped into sidewalk cement at construction sites, undiscovered suicide pacts, lost manuscripts, perfectly imagined gold medal attempts, cracks in wine glasses that spell your name after you throw them out, walkie-talkies with nobody on the other end.

≣

When I got home, Derek was leaning over the TraceBox™, scrubbing Wink's shell with a toothbrush.

"Hey," I said.

"Good morning."

I fixed myself a breakfast of Red Bull, bagels, and wasabi cream cheese. I looked around for paint smudges, smeared palettes, a full ashtray—any kind of evidence that Derek was being creative, and that I was being a good muse and delivering my half of the deal. Instead, I saw the piles of magazines that he had apparently begun to sort by title.

Hmmm.

"Maybe I forgot to tell you that you could sleep here as well," Derek said, polishing Nod with a squirt of Colgate.

"I got a modeling job last night at the club."

"Good for you."

He was scrubbing like they teach you, in little circles.

"Derek, you told me to go there," I said.

"I know."

He turned and smiled at me.

"I'm happy for you. I was wondering when you'd move up in the food chain."

Even if he was being sincere, the rest of my bagel and cream cheese tasted like paper and mud. There are some things you just don't say.

"What did you think of Jason?" he said.

"You fucking set us up?"

"Please don't swear so much. I wanted you to get a good gig, but—"

"I can't *believe* you."

"—but I was expecting you to come home last night. That's all."

Because graffiti is among the most expensive art forms, because art matters, because movies aren't called movies, they're called films, because the rats underground are bigger than most dogs on Central Park West, because you can fall asleep on a Brooklyn-bound D train and wake up at the ocean.

I wasn't surprised when I walked into alt.coffee and saw Chase screaming on the floor, re-enacting his famous scene for an audience staring indifferently over their cappuccino foam.

"Aaaaaaaggghhhh! Just gimme back my legs so I can walk to school!"

A rush of keyboard clicks from the counter. Forest was surfing the Internet, proving that being earthcore didn't exclude you from the wonders of 90s technology.

"Listen to this," she said. "According to this fansite, when you feed Chase's scream into an oscillograph—"

"Aaaaaaaggghhhh! I promise I'll run to school!"

"—and turn it into a sound wave, it has the exact same sonic peaks as an earthquake after fall equinox."

She turned to Chase and melted. "Baby, you're like, totally seasonal."

"No, I'm not. I'm Hollywood. Hey, mister writer."

I helped him up.

"How's the novel?" he said.

That diamond-cut smile. I could tell he was trying.

"It was a short story, and it got rejected."

"Was it a form letter?"

"It got pretty personal."

"That's fantastic."

"Don't humiliate him," Forest said.

"I'm being serious," Chase said. "It wasn't a form letter, so it means they love him, sort of."

"They like you," Forest said to me. "Almost."

Chase clapped his hand on my shoulder.

"You're one step closer to making a movie. Isn't that why you write, so they'll make a movie out of it?"

As Chase carefully repositioned a strand of hair, I drank the bitter grinds of my coffee and wondered why I hung out with these two. They were like the residual flashes that followed a lightning storm— in your face, but superfluous.

Forest was being quiet and weird. She glanced at my crotch, gave me a smirk, then tilted the computer screen so she could be alone with it.

Something was up.

I suddenly felt like I was back in the Williamsburg elevator—light and unreal.

"Show it to me," I said.

She turned the screen that changed my day from mediocre to rotten:

I recognized the La-Z-Boy, the Lego coffee table, my kink of pubic hair. Images, frames. Everything was backwards. Someone had re-arranged time, shifting events around like they were Post-it notes.

I piss in a glass.

I drink the liquid.

I give the world my saddest face.

The website was called *Forced to Guzzle*.

Holy tit-clamping Mother of God.

"Dude," Chase said, "if you're into drinking your own piss, then you *have* to make a movie."

And suddenly there was a photographer out there I wanted to murder. I think his name was Brent. Or maybe Raoul. And Derek was going to get it, too.

I got another envelope today.

The return address was *Zoetrope All-Story* magazine, the brainchild of Francis Ford Coppola, a fifty-pager that made careers. Getting published in *Zoetrope* supposedly made you famous and got you catered luncheons where the wine had a cork, not a screw top.

The envelope was crisp and done up in Helvetica letterhead. I didn't open it right away, wanting to savor the letter before it could hurt me.

But I was feeling pretty confident about the latest submission. I had taken my time to flesh it out, then deconstruct it and put it back together, checking to see if the character was strong enough to rematerialize intact. I spent many afternoons in Barnes and Noble (yeah, now they let me in) poring over writing guides, learning what malapropisms will get you rejected at first glance, what kind of dialogue will make a character sound hollow, the importance of interior monologue, and how to avoid pulling punches that need to hit hard.

I tightened my grammar, plotted my story arcs for effective build-up and release, and memorized successful query letters word-for-word. I did my homework.

Oh, but that was not enough.

You cannot lay genius to paper, page fifty-two of *The UnFrustrated Writer* says, if you are not in a suitably controlled environment.

Tompkins Square Park in the East Village was ideal, specifically because of the maze-like layout that disoriented me just enough to get me lost in the story, and because I had to hop a fence and disobey a Parks Department sign to get to the shady patches of grass.

You cannot write heroically if you live a take-no-chances, conventional life, page thirty-nine says.

I found solidarity in watching other writers disappear into their notebooks. We kept each other in check, stopped each other from floating away to the distractions of spring.

I wrote my story.

The kid was sick of being force-fed Ritalin, coerced with pills into moods that overwhelmed him and followed him around like cloud cover. Nobody had the right to control his interior weather like that.

He decided to strike back.

He learned how to fake taking his pills, and built up a secret stash that he gradually introduced into his parents' food supply. Noodles were the perfect camouflage for pills because he could noodle them in, and so was hot soup because they melted. The kid now cooked breakfast, lunch, and dinner for his parents, and did it with pleasure.

While they floated through the world in a forced state of being "with it," the kid got back to the business of living. He discovered other ways of focusing, treatments that the adult world didn't recognize. He found that by sneaking close to his sleeping father and palming one of his huge testicles, turning it around and documenting its shape, color, texture, and smell, he could plug into the realities of life.

Then he would put it away and try to imagine it. On good days, his brain could turn his father's testicle into a 3-D egg bobbing in his head. The wormy tubes, the pubic dusting, the filigree veins. It was pleasurable to wrap his mind around something so tangible. He found other objects to focus on, not all of them in his father's underwear.

Perhaps he had fed his parents too much Ritalin, because they began to vomit, convulse, soar through euphoria, drool through delirium, and experience heart palpitations.

By the time his parents realized what was going on, the kid had built up such an arsenal of useful and comforting objects in his mind that when they shipped him off to reform school, he knew he would be able to cope.

Dear Mr Marshall,
Thank you for submitting your story, Cerebral Immunity.

After careful consideration, we have decided not to publish it. The story is well written, but doesn't seem plausible enough to justify the level of intimacy you encourage between the reader and the protagonist. We need to be absolutely convinced that this really happened to the character.

Also, we do not publish paedophilia.

Feel free to send us more of your work, and best of luck with your writing endeavors.

The Publishers

The envelope was, but the envelope is no more.

It is unlikely that you will become a published author, page seventy-five of the *UnFrustratedWriter* says, if you hold on to your failures.

"I notice you're not too interested in paying the rent we agreed on," Derek says.

"*Forced to Guzzle*," I say.

"I didn't know he was going to do that."

"Can't wait for the sequel. Any other friends of yours I should work with? Anyways, it's not like you need the money."

"That's right," he says. "Turtle paintings are all the rage right now."

"I hate it when you're like that."

"Pulling your own weight. That's all this is about."

"You should talk. I see the checks your mom sends."

"That's different," he says. "We have an arrangement."

I wouldn't have learned how to ride the subway for free if they hadn't revealed the secret in the *Daily News*. There was this guy who had figured out how to bend MetroCards in just the right place, creasing a mysterious point in the magnetic strip to romance the turnstiles forever. He hadn't paid a fare in years. When they finally caught him, he was wearing a brass knuckles–type ring that fit across all four fingers, with the word TRANSIT spelled out in diamonds. Paid for, supposedly, with the money he had saved on subway fare.

The day I read the article, I scavenged a stack of old MetroCards, sat in the corner of a subway entrance, and put them through a fork until I bent one just right.

Ka-ching.

I was supposed to change trains downtown to go see this photographer guy (the back of the *Village Voice* is a goldmine), but I dozed off. I dreamt about someone sitting me on a dinner table and bending me different ways through a fork until my services were indefinitely free. I remember squeezing through the metal prongs, escaping just in time, though I couldn't see who had been doing the bending.

"LASTSTOPLASTSTOPLASTSTOP, everbodyouteverybodyout."

By the time I pried my drooling jaw off the Dr Zizmor ad (dermatological celebrity—you don't want to know), I was the last one left on the train. I ran for the doors and dove out just as they were closing.

The ocean. Although it's always in the same place, Coney Island is always a surprise.

The ocean ended at the sand, and the sand kept Astroland Amusement Park from sliding into the water.

The Cyclone: A screaming rollercoaster bristling with arms, hoisted on termite-eaten stilts the width of matchsticks. All bend and creak, this death trap. Perhaps it changed you by displacing your center of gravity to outside your body, to the top of the track where you took your last breath.

The Wonder Wheel: The Ferris mothership, spinning like a giant hamster wheel, offering you the freedom of the open sky, a place to make out and puke while locked in a cage. Perhaps it changed you by giving you infinite power that you could do nothing with.

The Astrotower: The best place to watch carnies scamming dollar bills, moms rifling paintballs at clowns, vendors trawling the beach with cotton candy and Heineken, New Jersey prom queens noshing hot dogs, and kids riding mattresses lost at sea.

Perhaps the rides only changed you when they broke down and stranded you, hanging there, high above nothing you'd care to return to.

The best rides, the ones that didn't move, were gone. I could hear echoes of Dreamland, where the world had come so many years ago to sway motionless, ogle the million light bulbs, and marvel over the wonders of electricity. When the bulbs shorted out and the wonders of electricity set fire to the zoo, these people ran screaming from the flaming zebras and tigers that were escaping into Brooklyn.

Running from lions with manes of fire.

I left Astroland and got lost in the noise of Surf Avenue, past a newsstand where Russians were screaming at soccer on TV. I came to a sign that said *Shit and Ephemera* and ducked inside, and by the time I figured out that they did tattoos, a woman had handed me a white towel.

"Trash it."

"I don't work here."

"Who says I'd hire you? Anyways, what do you want? Let me guess, the Ramones on your ass."

"Actually, no."

I examined the towel.

"Tell me this is blood."

"Crucifixion Crimson, made to look like the inside of Christ on impalement day. You want some?"

She held her tattoo gun over the empty chair.

"I'd like to see a catalogue, please."

She rolled her eyes and gave me a black binder spilling with images. It didn't take me long to find something I liked, something representative, a tattoo that chose me as much as I chose it. Something to remind me of Coney Island when I was trapped in the city.

"Hmmh," she said.

She wrapped the flames around my waist, lick by lick. Fire cannot be counted, and neither can animals when they swarm you. Orange, yellow, and red melded in infinite measures. That's how it is with life. With pain, I mean.

Every day I look at my tattoo and it reminds me that whatever I do below the waist usually causes me pain. The shitty part is that no two burns are the same, so I can never steel myself beforehand.

At least I didn't return to Manhattan the same boy.

I found myself on the sixth floor of a Tribeca walk-up, out of breath and staring at the door, wondering what this address I had culled from the wanted ads was going to make me do.

He opened the door. Fifty-five, fifty-six, a wizened man with eyes of blue crystal, white goatee and hair buzzed short, a body that had grown comfortable with itself. I usually get hard around these daddy types, but this one had a different vibe.

"Right, I'm Richard Rorschach, so you're here, so tell me about yourself."

"I don't do Internet shoots, and I don't drink piss," I said.

He gave me a hurt look.

"Don't worry, we're not going to do that, so I just want you to relax. There's no pressure, right? Tell me about your day."

I figured he was just pulling a chatty routine to get me to shuck, so to save us both some time I gave him the merchandise right off. I had already developed a little stripping act: flex my biceps and toss my bangs, unfurl my T-shirt over my head, stare into space like I was reconsidering, then insolently kick off my Fiorucci sneakers like I'd rather be at the dentist. They crash-landed into an aloe vera plant in the corner. I had yet to perfect the finer points.

"What are you doing?" he said.

"Just wait."

I cocked my head, gave him the Jaeven lip sneer, undid my belt buckle, and let my jeans fall to the floor. I turned around and spread 'em. I spread those cheeks so wide that if I had farted just then, it would've been a sigh.

"Come on, you don't have to do that, it's not you."

"You don't know anything about me."

"If you were a plastic go-go boy, you would've checked yourself in the mirror by now. Like, come on, right? So go get your shoes and show me the real you."

I fetched my sneakers, bent an aloe tentacle back into place, and returned to Richard. He led me into a pale blue, nearly empty living room, though it was big enough to be a studio.

I watched my hands as they began to move, tying and untying the dirty shoelaces. I had walked this city inside out in these shoes, picking up scuffmarks and lessons along the way.

"Look at you, that's it."

"What?"

"Whatever you're doing. You're being you."

"Who else would I be?"

"Right, yeah, well some people can't be themselves."

And in that moment, I felt naked for the first time in my life, as silly as that sounds. I had never felt so vulnerable before, or so beautiful. My tattoo was oozing, and it hurt me tender and deep.

It felt like I had just bumped my head against the wooden walls of my TraceBox™.

Richard had become a lens, the lens of a boxy Hasselblad camera mounted on a tripod. It was an old-fashioned clunker that hid him quite well.

"So tell me your story, tell me about the shoes. I like to sniff around old stuff. You know, I'm a goat. But I promise not to eat them."

I felt stupid for not having noticed their condition before. The white leather high-tops had been worked supple and raw, and so had the textile inlay with the Fiorucci logo. I had missed a shoelace eyelet on each one. The soles were worn down unevenly and made me wonder if I had a limp I didn't know about. There was bubble gum stuck in the treads.

It was painfully quiet in the room.

With Richard, there was no music.

"Tell me the story," he said again.

"They came with my first apartment."

"Talk to me about where these shoes have been."

I looped a butterfly knot and told him everything—the places in New York where trouble had picked up my scent and followed me, the places where I had seen proof that the human will is stronger than any poison the world can feed it, the places that had changed me forever, and the places I would rather forget.

These shoes, for better or for worse, had brought me to where I was. It sounds stupid and simplistic, but it's so true.

He clicked and snapped. I didn't feel naked anymore, because I realized that he was shooting me, not my body.

I was surprised when Richard gave me three hundred dollars—it didn't feel like we'd done anything. He picked up my sneakers and untied the laces for me.

"You don't shoot porn," I said.

"Plastic go-go boys don't interest me. Come back in a few weeks and bring something else for show and tell."

"I have a baseball cap."

"As long as it's not new, you know I'm a goat."

He stuck his nose in my sneakers, took a few pleasure snorts, and gave them back to me.

"Right," he said.

I've gotten used to seeing Derek's back when I open the door to the loft. Square shoulders that shift and straighten when I click the door shut. I think he likes me walking in on him, catching him doing whatever.

Based on certain patterns of coexistence, I have reason to believe that he never leaves home anymore. It's equally plausible that he spends as much time out-of-doors as I do, and our paths are hard-wired to overlap only in the loft. And even then, sometimes we'll only see each other a few times a day: in bed, by the window, trading places in the bathroom.

"Hi, Booger," he said. "There's some eggplant parmigiana in the oven. Pepper's in the grinder."

"Booger? Am I another one of your pets?"

"Don't get testy. It's just what ... what people do."

At first I thought that he was hanging up the latest turtle-trace canvas, but no.

He was painting.

Derek Brathwaite was creating, without the aid of reptiles. Mixing paint, cocking his head at the canvas on the easel, muttering incomplete words under his breath, dabbing, shading, and sighing. He had a brush in each hand and daubs of paint on his shirt and face. I felt a surge of guilt, like I was interrupting a most delicate process that could disintegrate at any moment.

Wink and Nod were roaming free, exploring nooks and crannies, finding caves where there were none before.

Derek shot me a loaded look. If I had to venture a guess, it told me about a valve he had bust open, a drain he had unclogged, a lid he had lifted. It was a miracle to finally see him in his element. Sure, I had been a part of this release, but he owned this moment with a singularity that changed his whole demeanor. He had the body language of a man who felt free to be dangerous.

"You're doing it," I said, feeling like Richard Rorschach.

"Yes, I am ... You never come home with bruises anymore, so you've taken away my reason to procrastinate."

"I was worried you might miss my injuries."

"Not really."

I noticed my notebook lying on the bed. I didn't remember leaving it there, and even if I did, I wouldn't have left it open. I often bounce literary ideas off Derek, but I never let him see my writing. For some reason, it's okay to share it with magazine editors, but it's too personal to share with Derek.

Huge, impressionist swipes of magenta. Agitated swirls where a hand would be. I moved in closer to his easel. He took a step back to let me soak it in, one stroke at a time. Charcoal ellipses, the outlines of plates on a dinner table. A looming figure made of layers of color, layers that looked like you could peel them back. Hazy, Monet-like washes hiding the brightest blue flame.

A handful of pills.

My latest story, told in acrylic.

"I'd like to talk about your jealousy problem," I said.

"What the FUCK are you talking about?"

"Why did you go through my notebook? What were you looking for?"

"Listen, Jaeven, you left it open. What was I supposed to do, pretend I hadn't read the first couple of lines? It was already too late. Your story hooked me and then I read the whole thing and realized it's what I've been looking for all along."

"You don't trust me."

"Why can't you be happy for me? You have everything you want," he said.

"I know it eats you up inside when I turn a trick or do a photo shoot. All I'm trying to do is make a living."

"Are you listening to yourself, Jaeven Marshall? We don't even have sex. How can I be jealous?"

"I know, that's what's weird about it."

"Right."

Derek wiped his forehead, smearing even more paint on himself. Nod was bumping into the jet engine, backing up, and making a metallic clunk with every go of it.

Maybe I was being a paranoid jackass, or maybe he actually mistrusted me. Whatever the case, I couldn't blame him for getting attached to me after all this time, and for feeling lonely when I was out gallivanting naked in the city. And I had to start accepting a certain loss of privacy that came with being in a relationship, as annoying as it was.

"Sorry," I said.

"That's okay."

He put down his brushes.

"It's the first time I've ever seen you paint," I told him.

"It is," he said.

"Your first show is going to be amazing."

He dabbed a splotch of purple on the tip of my nose.

Now that I think about it, I'm not worried about Derek reading my short stories. He's bound to read them eventually, since I plan to publish them. That is, if the universe conspires to keep me alive long enough.

It bugs me only mildly that he might discover the Coney Island I wrote about, that I might lose my secret hiding place.

But it drills a hole in my head, day and night, wondering if he read the other stuff. What I wrote about him. It makes me sick, thinking about how he'd react to the way I've been characterizing him as a gentle romantic with opaque moods I try to crack. He might be uncomfortable in that box. He might feel weak.

Or worse yet, he might think that I'm in love with him.

Part 2

I PASSED A HOMELESS KID on Eighth Avenue today, twenty-two, twenty-three, looking scruffier than he had to. It's freaking summertime and he was wearing a winter jacket with rips in it, when there are shelters all over the city that give clothes away for free.

It's easy to steal disposable razors, so he has no excuse for the two-week beard. And as for his nappy hair, all he has to do is run a restroom faucet—tap water in New York is the cleanest in the world.

Couldn't he have hustled a room by now, a mildly compromising living situation, anything? A Prada liquidation center? He's crouching in a doorway under a pile of torn cardboard when he could be on the beach under the stars, eating hot dogs and clams for free.

This kid clearly has no skills. Put me back on the street and I'd have all the details worked out within a week, I swear.

I took a free subway to Broadway and Houston today and had a meeting with Phil McDougall, lord and emperor of the gay porn magazine world.

It was intimidating walking down the hallway to his office, through a gauntlet of framed magazine covers all tilted down to make you feel small and unimportant if you weren't up there among the nudie idols.

Honcho: The magazine for bears, bear-cubs, and the men who love them. Leather cross-straps, cigars, neck tattoos, and young turks with enough facial hair to ruin their boyish glee. Furry patches moistened with spit, hairy asses spread on pool tables, reluctant manly cherries, five-o'clock shadows, chains, dangling cigarettes, dark mischief, rimming, spit wads all by themselves, muscles, military deviance, revolvers, and pissed-on jock straps.

It's actually a less cliché read than it sounds.

Inches: The magazine for size queens and those who get off on being consumed by envy. Rulers, measuring tapes, yardsticks, fisheye lenses, awe-inducing perspective, heft, swing, low-hangers, miles of shaft, off-the-page, white lies that nobody minds, foreskin fetishes, growers, curves, bulges, packages, centerfolds you want to ride to the moon, big dicks on little twink boys that make them look ridiculous and irresistible, Latino chulos.

Black Inches: See above, but black.

Playguy: The magazine for candy twinks and those addicted to their fruit-loop flavors. Bubble butts, twist-on/twist-off smiles, dimples, dorm-room play dates, popsicles, lollipops, sparkles and eye shadow, low-slung belts, hairless cracks, shaved pubes, Photoshop, coyness, fake ID cards, undies, go-go boys, parental consent, frolicking poolside with slender dildos, lip gloss, loose shorts, puppy dog love, necklaces and bracelets, pacifiers.

I wanted it all. Not because pornstar was my preferred career choice, but because it would pay enough to give me time to write. I was sure that publishers, no matter their stripe, all hung out together. I could use my porn fame to make connections that would get my fiction published. The challenge was to become everyone's perfect whore without taking myself too seriously.

Phil walked me over to his Wall of Polaroids.

"Do you know what it takes to become Boy New York?"

I looked at the thousands of awkward, posing boys and bit my tongue because I was about to answer "ugly." I didn't want to spoil my big chance, so I tried to be innocent and cute by saying nothing and giving him nonchalant eyes. He returned to his desk.

"You have to be magic, pure and simple."

I jumped on the desk, swept his Jeff Stryker dildo/paperweight to the floor, and reclined on one elbow.

"You know I deserve it."

"No one deserves anything. A lot of kids come to New York and make that mistake."

He had a nice shaved skull and drippy brown eyes that were either expressionless or consistently sad. I couldn't tell which.

"You mean if you weren't queen shit of this magazine empire that you wouldn't pay seven bucks to see me nude?"

"You're being cute," he said.

It was time for Plan B.

"You need a massage," I said.

I stretched Phil out on the floor and gave him what was probably the best workout of his life, a beating of the touchy-feely prescription.

He groaned an internal gush and went kind of limp.

"*Playguy*," I said. "Then *Honcho, Mandate, Inches*. Your timetable."

"Ooohhhhhhh fuck, that's good."

Some judo chops in his most brutally tender spots, the shoulder blades and kidneys. I worked past his softness and into bone.

"I have some creative ideas about how I'd like to pose."

"We'll have to see about that. When can you massage me next?"

"I'm not even finished and you're already talking about the next time?"

"It's just ..."

"Yeah, I know."

Saw it all the time. The hands of the young are murder on men in their thirties.

"I want to be in *Black Inches*," I said.

"Don't push it," Phil said. "We'll see."

I had to buy a better pager because business was picking up and it was rattling the life out of my old one. I upgraded to a transparent blue model with hip holster and Talking Heads ring tones. Cellphones are a turn-off to older guys who expect a more destitute hustler. I can't disappoint. Image is everything.

The pager either buzzes with numbers I know, with numbers I don't, or with codes I've given out but forget what they mean. Mixing up the codes is a dangerous business.

Here are some of them and the transactions they stand for:

0066—We meet at the Hilton Hotel at 9:30. You bring condoms, lube, vodka, cranberry juice, menthol cigarettes, coke, and $400 cash. I do as much blow as you like, suck you off, and fuck you. We watch infomercials all night and have a generally icy time. You toss in a fifty-dollar tip if I know where you work and how much you make.

0099—You can already see the confusion these numbers lead to. You need me to look pretty at a party with you. I gussy up your arm, make it look younger. I'm disinclined to say "arm candy" because I'm slightly hairy and not as Hollywood as the expression implies. We're a hot date and everyone knows it. Two hundred dollars is fine. No kissing.

0020—This one can vary. Either you want a blowjob in your car and I have to call you for the coordinates, or you want to fuck in a club bathroom. I get sketched out by 0020s, so I don't answer them unless I'm really hard up, which is more often than I care to admit.

0013—All I'm going to say is you'd better be fucking rich, gentle, and have no kids of your own. If you have a camera in the vicinity and I find it, I crack it over your head.

0052—Phil needs a massage, the darling. How could I say no?

Jaeven Marshall, twenty-two.

Here's my product description, the spin I have to believe in order to sell myself effectively.

Here's the press release.

Slacker hair and black bangs long enough to have fuck-you cachet. No pimples. I smell great. I climbed out of the puberty swamp a victor, with hormones riding that ideal balance. I've got blue eyes that you can stare through into oblivion, and a pierced lip so red you think it's bleeding.

This is what I have to shill.

Snake-bitten nipples, chewed on and spritzed with lemon juice. I've had to swear on a New World Translation Bible that I don't rouge them up. A fire-chain tattoo circles my waist, a touch of glam just above the field of play.

Body hair—now here's where I've got all the niches covered. I'm so bushy in places and hairless in others that I can't help but offer the best of both worlds.

I've got pit-hawks under each arm, long four-inchers you can bury your nose in, and a spray of pubes that frame a pretty spectacular area. I've got a good face of stubble, and a treasure trail running from my belly to ... oh, I'll tell you later.

The flip-side of me is the ass of a preteen boy, a sweet hairless crack buried deep between doughy bubble cheeks. My pink asshole is ringed with a brown stain, like icing I can never wipe off. The men, the customers, they drool over dichotomy, contrasts that make no sense in the world of physical development.

I'm an anomaly.

This is the stuff I have to believe, even though most of it isn't true.

Okay, moving down to the real merchandise.

When I shuck my pants, the first thing you'll see will be my cock, not only because it's darker than the rest of me, but because it's the wrong size. It's tiny.

Just kidding.

It's bleeping gi-normous. A man's dick on a boy's body. Eight inches you don't want to mess with, or you *do* want to mess with, as the case may be.

And that's the complete me. Clearly pedestal material. I've got to go now, and anyways, I'm not the type to talk about myself forever.

Because New York manholes hiss with steam even in summer, because men on tricycles lug around giant blocks of ice, scrape off shavings, then drown them in blueberry syrup and sell them, because firefighters in the Bronx bust open the hydrants so kids can splash away the heat, because sometimes you'll make the mistake of choosing a subway car where the air conditioning's broken and you'll want to kill somebody.

≋

I never expected to be in the Toilet Böys' lead singer's apartment. I'm not sure how this photographer chick Crystal Vase swung it.

"Yeah, show me some wood."

My cock's growing because of the punk band T-shirt framed on the wall. It's the one where Sean Pierce (screw him for having devil horns and making me attracted to a straight boy) is showing off his heaving dick. His glam punk band is famous, though, for other reasons. John Waters and Debbie Harry at every show? Fire-breathing finales and sex with the audience? It's got to be something.

Crystal sets up her lights and plays Duran Duran's "Hungry Like the Wolf." How does she know that's my mood track? Her lithe, little body is slinking in a purple leather catsuit. Doesn't talk a lot, but communicates the important stuff with dangerous eyes.

All these shenanigans we do with cameras.

The freeze.

The pose.

The hold and don't move.

The go crazy.

The show me more.

The back it up.

The spread it.

The work it.

The lie down.

The now turn.

The smile.

The scowl.

The beam.

The wince.

The grimace.

The look into the camera. The look beyond the camera.

Why do we waste our time dealing with people when we can deal with their photographs?

"Where's that wood? Move to the edge of the sofa, you rockstar."

These photogs like me because I'm obedient and creative. Billy Idol's "Dancing With Myself" comes on, and that's exactly what I do. I wipe my pits with my undies, twirl them around, squeeze my foreskin into a rosebud, and pretend to sit on a middle finger while pumping my other hand in the air to the music.

My fuck-you-but-fuck-me-too sneer. My fierce eyebrow arch. Let the people have what they want.

I've learned that attitude sells. There are better-looking guys out there, but they don't get this kind of attention because they don't know how to jam the viewer's emotions. Make him so weepy, he'll put his dick away and hug your magazine cover in bed until sunrise.

"Now show me where that cock belongs."

Classic. She knows I can do it. I wonder if this is the ultimate in narcissism, but who really gives a shit? It's all for the writing. I assume the position, propping my butt against the sofa back, scooting my hips over my head. I stare at my tattoo.

This is the only way to end these photo shoots. To go up in flames.

I plant my knees on either side of my head. I can feel the blood draining from my dick, rushing behind my eyes. Crystal notices the disturbing softness and pads over stealthily. She squeezes her fist expertly around the base of my cock and brushes a finger across my asshole. She's too good at this. Word has it she's a dominatrix by night. I throb and inch it closer to my face.

I've never done this before. Extend. The tip's at my lips, then deeper, then I close around my mushroom head. It's warm, fat, and all very flattering. I can taste the zing of something about to happen.

"This is it. Shoot yourself in the head with that weapon, and try not to spill. Who's doing this to you, hon?"

She knows damn well who's doing it. I look up in worship at the gargantuan poster dick above me.

"Sean is."

And that's all I can say before I shoot cum down my throat, while Crystal snaps the shots I hope no one will bring out to my book signings as a practical joke.

I have to come clean with you again. I never figured out how to bend a MetroCard to make it work forever, but I told you I did because I needed a superpower to make you believe in me. I had to convince you that I could rise above the shit of life, and that I could do it in style. I hope that knowing this won't change your impression of me.

You know, sooner or later, you're going to have to share some secrets with me, or I might have to stop trusting you.

I might have to shut up.

Yesterday, there was an event.

I called Derek's painting "infantile."

You have to understand: there are two million words, all of them inappropriate, that I'm capable of saying at any minute of the day, to all the wrong people.

He misunderstood me.

The idea is this: words tick, fizzle, and explode in my mouth if I don't let them out.

Open a grammar book and you'll see a list of my heavy artillery: impersonal pronouns, punctuating adjectival clauses, gerunds and infinitives, paired conjunctions, modifying adverbial phrases, transitions, mixed conditionals, prepositions, modal auxiliaries, uncountable nouns, comparatives and superlatives, transitive verbs.

I have a particular problem with garden-variety adjectives.

Trapping them in, I feel the combustion building up, and then when my tongue blasts flapping out of my mouth, there's no telling what I'll say. Even worse, in polite social situations when I have to swallow these dangerous subject-verb-object combinations (which often seem quite harmless to me), my stomach's at full blowout risk.

I called his painting "infantile," but I meant to say "innocent." Is that the worst crime in the world?

Screw vocabulary.

Gem Spa on First Avenue is the coolest bodega I know, and not only because they have the biggest magazine selection in the East Village, or because they have those quirky red-and-white striped paper cups that you can't find anywhere else.

It's because of the clientele, but not who you think.

Liza Minnelli on one of her midnight benders? Who cares.

Alec Baldwin getting a *New York Post* and flipping to the Page Six gossip column so he can remember what he did the night before? Old news.

Susan Lucci mapping news clippings of herself into some kind of astrological chart to predict when her second Daytime Emmy Award win will be? As if.

These and other washed-up stars lurk around in semi-transparent shades, checking to see if they can still make the magazine covers. The glasses are semi-transparent because they want to be recognized, of course, while they still can.

No, Gem Spa's main attraction is somebody entirely different.

Celebrity photog, image-maker, master of the beautifugly: David LaChurch.

May's covers are stacked in a grid of risers—a magazine altar. I want to lick the fruit-loop ink right off them because they celebrate everything I hold dear about hard luck. David LaChurch is the only photographer who can make a candy-coated masterpiece out of the sheep manure that life slings at you.

The Face: Drew Barrymore in a banana yellow waitress's uniform, sprawled on the floor of a typical New Jersey diner, miles away from the set of E.T., one perky breast hanging out amid spilled grapefruit and maraschino cherries. She's wearing a cutout paper tiara made for the disposable age.

Details: Leonardo DiCaprio, post-Titanic but looking pre-pubescent, bleeding sexily under a crown of thorns. His lips are so red, it's either lip-gloss or blood. There's something quintessentially New York about glorifying little-boy masculinity. There's something hopelessly LA about a corrupted Beverly Hills brat striking a Jesus pose.

It disgusts me that these actors know nothing about the hardship they're portraying, but at least they're trying to make it look real.

Rolling Stone: Trent Reznor with his lips sewn shut, lying on a bed of white fur. Cheap, silver-painted Realistic microphone for the Lo-Fi age. Everybody knows there's no way to shut Reznor up, so we'll chalk it up to LaChurch's meticulous airbrushing team.

Interview: The hotel room is washed Pepto-Bismol pink. An overweight Courtney Love look-alike in a pink Chantilly lace prom dress and messy lipstick. She's serving a rat on a silver platter to a faux "Girlie Show"-era Madonna (in a wheelchair, no less) who's smoking a set of wrinkles into herself. Nipple tassels for the age of the young-at-heart, when you can be anyone in the world. Not that you'd want to.

Paper: Lily Tomlin in a fern-choked forest, sitting on a giant spotted mushroom, using a lichen for a footstool. The spots make her mottled complexion look amazing by comparison. She sips, shell-shocked and staring into the camera, from a straw stuck in a red-and-white striped Gem Spa cup.

Spin: Tom Jones in a hot pink catsuit, hanging off the mirror bracket of an eighteen-wheeler that's stopped in front of an inflatable Uniroyal tire the size of a house. The gayest straight man in pop music (aside from Ricky Martin) is singing to the vanishing point on the road in front of him. An anthem for the lost and misguided.

The Advocate: It makes sense that a celebrity photographer is his own best model. David himself in a boxing ring, looking bruised but defiant, swatting at invisible ghosts who shadow-punch him. Good metaphor for how the pundits get on his case about taking vacuous pictures of nothing, and him hustling past those who can't appreciate the nothingness of life.

May is a Technicolor sweep. I hear that David's making a film, something to pull us all deeper into LaChurch Land. I can hardly wait for these covers to come to life.

Then I see it.

It looks right at home, nestled between Leonardo and Trent.

Playguy: Jaeven Marshall in a concrete half-pipe, sprawled topless in skintight grass-stained jeans, holding a skateboard between his open legs. If you focus real hard, you can almost see the wheels spinning. Baseball cap cocked to the indigo sky, middle finger sprouting from a hand scraped red and raw. Shadows play with the contours of his crotch. A hero for the can't-give-a-shit.

These tiny shards of chemical glass that I swish into cans of Red Bull (sometimes it's a yellowish powder that smells like cat pee—every bathtub lab is different) is finally creeping into New York. They say it has already eaten up all the young gay men on the West Coast, and now it needs new blood. They say it makes us unsafe, makes us fuck each other without condoms. It wastes us until we turn into gargoyles and paw at each other's deformed faces. Friends become impossible to recognize, so they say.

Whatever.

Some people are oblivious to the fact that there are always two ways to spin something, that every side effect has an equal and opposite benefit. Some people are stupid. Most of them, actually.

It's very simple. ADD takes my alertness away. Crystal meth gives it back. The universe takes care of itself.

A lot of kids smoke it, but that's too junkie for me, and snorting has never been my trip. Sure, meth can make you sick if you drink too much of it, and some people have to get their stomach pumped. I'm not like that, though. I would rather stick my fingers down my throat than visit a hospital. They take your drugs away in there, believing the media hype.

Anyways, it was all I could do to get through a Richard Rorschach photo shoot and have me be anything but a blur. He's too intense for me.

"Look at you, right."

Richard dipped the tea bag in his cup like he was going fishing.

"You're still beautiful," he went on. "New York has had its paws all over you and you still shine."

I wondered if he could see my teeth chatter and my eyes go squiggly. He was expecting me to say something.

"Right," I said.

Richard led me to a work table, gave me a magnifying loupe, and slid a row of negatives on the light tray, as neatly and meticulously as he did everything.

It was from the last photo shoot. I had gone crazy with a roll of masking tape, fashioning myself a coat of beige adhesive armor, then a baseball uniform, then binding and gagging myself. A knight, an athlete, a prisoner: masking tape versions of people I've wanted to be, each of them heroic in their own special way.

"It's amazing how many different Jaevens can be convincingly you. You're the real deal."

"I see."

Richard pressed my hand on the light tray like a cop taking fingerprints.

"Yeah, right, look."

When a light flushes your skin, your skin turns into glowing rice paper. Your veins pulse red and translucent. The mystery of you disappears, and so does the fear. Richard was the real light box, and he shone brightly through me every time I was with him.

"So what are you going to give me today?"

Thank God Richard didn't shoot porn.

I tore the cushions off his couch and threw them on the floor. This was going to go down as planned, as I mapped it out when I was giving ass to a boring trick and I needed to escape cerebrally to a sixth floor in Tribeca.

"I'm going to show you what I feel like these days."

Cushioned thud. The weight of limbs. I fell on my face, all the while locking gaze with the camera lens, with Richard. I wanted him to capture the look in my eyes just before I hit the floor—what I imagined would be a creeping fearlessness. The look of young men when they realize they own the city they're enslaved to.

We shot a couple of rolls. There were no mirrors in Richard's place. I tried to picture what he saw that day, what gave him that slapped look of awe, what made him emerge from behind the lens and stare straight at me as I fell time and time again. Maybe he was seeing invisible bruises. There were real ones for sure, when my shoulder missed the cushion and slammed into the hardwood floor, but those aren't the kind that stay with you.

We finished and he snuck the film away to what I guessed was his darkroom. He came out after a while, pensive and quiet. I whipped out my notebook, lay shirtless on the floor, and started to write about Derek.

"I mean the pillows, right?" he said. "There's someone you trust or want to trust, so it was like, let's go there."

"I see them more as cushions."

"Whatever, come on."

"You're still way off."

"I mean, your face was like, hello?"

"Maybe a little."

"Okay, good. Because you should just let it happen. Do you mind if I shoot? Why don't I get you a tea?"

"Whatever. Sure."

"Don't stop what you're doing," he said. "It's cool."

Our relationship changed. From that day on, I went to Richard's to write, he shot, and he brought me a piping cup of jasmine tea roughly every four pages.

≡

One of the massages that made me famous:

Full Swedish treatment including muscle pulverization. Phil cried like a little boy.

Inches cover, June 1999. Phil convinces Lower East Side photog Richard Kern that there is more to erotic photography than anorexic junkie girls with track marks on their cooch. We hop the fence to an abandoned amphitheatre in Riverside Park that's covered in graffiti. I hang rat traps from my foreskin for full extension.

Fan letter to *Inches*, July 1999:

> Dear *Inches*,
> Thank you for finally printing a picture of a guy I can keep in my wallet. What a hunk! Can you tell him that I just want to hold his dick against my face when it's soft and kiss his foreskin? Better yet, can you pack him and his big beautiful dick up in a suitcase and post him to Brighton? We English lads will treat him right (as if!) and we'll make sure to send him back in one piece. Every time I look into his deep blue eyes I get this feeling of total surrender.
> And I'm already stocking up on rat traps!
> Bill in Brighton, England

As a person who is often photographed, I will now posit an interpretation of selected quotes from Susan Sontag's *On Photography*, a book I stole from some trick's shitter:

"To collect photographs is to collect the world ... To photograph is to appropriate the thing photographed."

Wow. Bang on. Sometimes I wonder if Susan Sontag was a hustler boy in a previous life. For aging Manhattan art fags, the next best thing to a night with me is a picture of me. They want to own me, take me home with them, imprison me behind glass, and then jerk off carefully. Putting something behind glass speeds up the disidentification process. You can only fetishize somebody you can't relate to, and the best way to make that happen is to dehumanize them, turn them into a two-dimensional copy. Drain the fluids, and suck out the personhood so it doesn't stink up the display case.

"Photographic images do not seem to be statements about the world so much as pieces of it."

When photographers ask me to sign prints of myself, I understand what this is about. Personalization. A DNA imprint. What is called "realia" in academic circles. So I lick the corner, gob it up with snot, leave a smudge of pre-cum or a bloody fingerprint. Do they want a piece of me or not?

"Photographs furnish evidence."

Evidence of me.

I was here.

I existed.

I was totally hot.

People felt things when I fucked them.

I made people cum.

I made people happy.

I was ignored.

My brain was never validated.

I'm too beautiful to write something deep.

I'm too naked to be a writer.

I'm too exposed to be published.

I'm a raving ADD case, if you haven't already noticed. I have a hell of a time recording dates and places and situating myself in a timeline of events that may or may not have happened. Sometimes the only way to know what I've done and where I've been is to flip to HX magazine's Who's Who society pages to find my drunken face laughing off the page, stumbling out of a club I can recognize from the décor and the tricks holding me up.

"The camera record incriminates."

You said it, philosophy sister. This is a partial list of things I've been caught doing on camera:

Swiping photo equipment for easy resale (never from Richard), sliding a broken condom out of a model's ass and smiling at the goo, blowing my meth dealer in a bathroom stall (the stuff is hard to find), posing with an intense pile of trash (hour forty-seven of a dumpster-diving adventure), punching out the photographer.

That's why it's useless to have a pseudonym. Slap whatever name you want on the picture, it's still me.

"There is an aggression implicit in every use of the camera."

Susan has obviously never met Richard Rorschach.

No, I don't talk about crystal meth a lot. Would you? The world is full of judgmental people ready to label you an addict, conveniently forgetting the substances they funnel into their own bodies, and the reasons they do it. Maybe you're one of them.

Like you've never loaded up on sugar to keep depression from dragging you down. You have never saturated your bloodstream with caffeine to give yourself just one more hour, frantically wasting another sixty minutes of your life. You have never been swimming in so much alcohol that drowning sounded like a fun proposition.

You have never worshipped a little cylindrical god packed with nicotine, pausing before you lit it to make sure you had at least one more left.

You have never used another person as a tool to hit that orgasmic sweet spot.

In the words of my friend Richard: yeah, right.

Another reason I don't talk about it is because it's impossible to describe how tweaking feels. I can say that when I shovel a thumb of meth into a can of Red Bull for midnight breakfast, it coasts into me like it's riding in a limousine, but you won't understand unless you've done it. I can say that there's a little animal that tickles me with its furry hooves, but it would be meaningless. You won't understand the high of staying up for three days straight and rooting through trash cans for fun things to take apart, like inferior shoes held together with glue. You won't understand the thrill of watching the city from a distance—the morning coffee scramble, the screams and fights and sales pitches, the squeals and crashes and depressed laughing, the scrape of shoes and tires, the drunken yawns and stumbling home—and being immune to it all.

It's impossible to explain what being a vampire feels like.

The main reason I don't talk about it, though, is because I'm not addicted. There's a difference between a user and an abuser. I know better than to let a drug take over my life.

Guys I'd like to fuck:

Lower East Side nihilists, twenty-four, twenty-five. Subdermal implants and other body modification that fucks with the social order one patch of skin at a time. Pants slung low on the hips, and truck mud flaps sewn on the ass, dragging down six inches of crack as a statement. Trucker hats are their only nod to pop culture. They stomp around with this sexy look on their face like they would rather you committed suicide. Inexplicable yet pleasingly macho fascination with trucks.

Computer geeks, nineteen, twenty. Tall, lanky, hunching around with laptops underarm. The sexy rings under their eyes attest to long nights trawling for Internet porn. Don't get enough sunlight to grow their patchy facial hair more evenly. You can see their dangly cocks flopping commando-style in their pants, cocks as long as their nail-bitten typing fingers. They stink gloriously of B.O. and semen.

Queer-as-fuck goth boys. They hurt too beautifully.

I'm also a boyeurist and a bona fide homeless-sexual. The more scruffy and out-of-pocket, the better.

Shiatsu rub with circulatory something.

Honcho cover, July 1999. Gay life partners Kim and Rick shoot me in front of a giant American flag, combing my pubic hair, doting over me like I was their prize poodle. I'm wearing an army jacket that's so big it's falling off. I wrap myself in the flag and give them my toughest sneers. It's not military enough, so I have to wave around this black plastic revolver. After the shoot, they insist that I watch them have sex.

Weird.

Fan letter to *Honcho*, August 1999:

> Dear *Honcho*,
> Can I have Jaeven's email address? If not, please tell him
> that I served in Iraq in the Gulf War, and every day I prayed
> I would run into someone as hunky as him in the muni-
> tions shed or in the showers after all the other soldiers had
> left. When are you going to do a shower scene with him?
> I'm sure I'm not the only one who's asked. It would be
> great to see that ass all lathered up. I wouldn't mind being
> the one to do it for him! Congratulations on a job well
> done.
> Lynn in Sarasota, Florida

There are times when the money comes so easily that I want to flush
it down the toilet, just for the hell of it. See old Ben Franklin drown.
I swear.

But I never get the chance, because the money disappears all by
itself.

People are starting to talk about the end of the world. There's all
this buzz over a puny little acronym:

Y2K.

The year 2000 is going to bring a terrible virus, they say.

They say that when the clock strikes midnight, January 1, all those zeroes are going to infect the computers of the world, eat through their wiring. The computers will think it's 1900 and self-destruct, realizing that they won't have been invented yet.

I'm mixing my verb tenses, but I'm sure you see why.

The lights will go out and civilization will crumble. We'll be opening subway doors with our teeth, counting money by hand. We'll all become savages, playing violin and drawing on cave walls.

So why hasn't anyone invented this sooner?

I've already gotten a jump on Y2K to make sure it doesn't bite me in the ass:

Pager: I upgraded again, and got one that's Y2K-compliant. I can't afford to lose any business on New Year's, especially since it's the busiest night of the year.

Currency: Because the US is likely to be hit the hardest, the money's bound to be shit. I've converted most of my cash to Canadian, since Canada doesn't have that much electricity and Y2K won't be a big deal for them.

Survival: Every time I steal pens from the pharmacy, I make a trip to Fiorucci and add them to the survival inventory I keep in the stock room, just in case. There are now about thirty notebooks, sixty candles, three boxes of matches, and forty packs of double-A batteries waiting for the day I'll need to disappear into music and write it all down.

Food: Stuff going bad all over the place. I'm looking forward to the world's biggest ice cream give-away.

Walkman: No upgrade required. The geniuses who invented analog must've seen the future.

≡

I was skeptical about doing a porn movie, especially when I found out that the producers were going to go the cliché way and make me a frigging pizza boy with red, red lips and an empty Domino's box. Screw that. But I needed the money and found a way to bend my mind around the indignities of playing a delivery person.

"Are you Jaeven?"

"It depends if you have money."

"Come in! Here's a drink."

"I'd rather pour it myself, if you don't mind."

"Well, he's been around the block, hasn't he?"

Ted and JohnSilas were this cutesy gay couple, JohnSilas a dark-haired, blue-eyed, puffy-chested Southern damsel and Ted a wry New Yorker with a busted nose and a ridiculous nose cast he was paranoid about people touching. They were the self-proclaimed New York extension of the Velvet Mafia, a porn empire based in San Diego. What an original name.

They introduced me to three nervous-looking twinks on the sofa:

Vince was an Asian kid with an eager smile, twenty, twenty-one, dressed in all-white casual wear from The Gap. The type of flake who took ten showers a day and had that perma-soap smell.

Miguel was a Latino dude, nineteen, twenty, a manicured thug with a Bronx bowl cut and Timberland boots. He lost street cred with me every time he bobbed his head.

Trey was a snotty little twink, seventeen, eighteen, who kept crossing and uncrossing his legs. He had a stuck-up face, the kind that could only be rearranged with a good smack.

We sat in a circle drinking Jägermeister on the rocks—Ted, JohnSilas, and I on stools in front of the twinks, waiting for the production crew to arrive. Awkward silence that we cut with random small talk. The Velvet Mafia had no idea how to set up a proper green room. Trey kept giving me these sickeningly coy little looks.

"Miguel, let's go get Trey cleaned up," Ted said, downing his drink.

"What do you mean?" Trey said. "I'm already clean."

"Have you done your enema yet?"

"What's that?"

It was official. Trey's brain was actually an airfield. Ted cupped his nose cast and shook his head.

"It's when you flush the shit out of your ass so it doesn't get stuck to the condom and make viewers puke when they watch your first video."

"Eww! That's gross."

They hustled Trey off to the bathroom and I wandered around. These guys were loaded. Wads of hundreds lying on the counter, real estate deeds for Florida condos in the fruit bowl, unused electronics spilling out of every cupboard. They clearly weren't making porn for the money, but at least now when they went to Milk, or Splash, or The Cock—I'd shoot myself if they started hanging out at Jackie 60—they could boast that the New York chapter of the Velvet Mafia actually did something.

"Here's a sock, handsome."

I nodded to JohnSilas, pretending that I knew what it was for, so I didn't look as dumb as Trey.

He opened the tanning bed and turned it on. Rows of squiggly, mauve UV bulbs lit up.

"We don't want you to sunburn your dick," he said.

First of all, I didn't see any sun in there. Secondly, I didn't know why they thought I needed a tan. And C, I couldn't figure out how they had gotten this cancerous contraption through the door.

"How long do you want me in there?"

"Till our star is nice and Hollywood. We're going to give you a Brooklyn accent when you do your monologue, but West Coasters won't pay for pasty skin. In general."

I shucked and got into the tanning bed, and was surprised to find it so comfy. It was nice to hide from the world inside a machine. There were headphones in there, so I put them on. Thomas Dolby was singing "She Blinded Me With Science," and it made my escape complete.

Ting.

"Time's up."

JohnSilas reset the egg timer and Miguel took my place. The Velvet Mafia decided to give me some time alone with the twink brood. I guess the idea was to let the wolf stir up the henhouse (or is the expression with a fox?) and then turn the cameras on just before the kill.

I circled Trey, sipping a vodka cranberry in just my underwear, showing off my bulge. Something in him brought out the latent predator in me, brought out my swagger. I was seeing mauve sunspots, so I must've appeared extra dodgy.

"You know that by the end of the night," I told Trey, "my dick's going to be up your ass. There's no avoiding it. Isn't it great how some things are just meant to be?"

I had been drinking too much.

"Huh. Whatever. We'll see what happens."

He wasn't flirting anymore. I could see a hangover starting to get to him, though he had been pretty good (like most teenagers are) at hiding the wear and tear.

I crunched an ice cube to scare him, but falling shards burned my over-cooked skin with their icy touch and made me jump instead.

"Is his ass nice and clean?" JohnSilas asked.

"As a whistle," Ted answered with a smirk that Trey didn't seem to appreciate.

We got down to business. I learned my lines and practiced them, channeling my best incarnation of a goofily sexy pizza boy for my shot at a Grabby Award and legendary status. The crew set up the lights and cameras, and scattered condoms and bottles of lube in convenient but hidden locations.

JohnSilas slipped a long blue horse-pill into my mouth and refreshed my drink. I must've let my guard down.

"Viagra. It'll help our star feel frisky."

I was about to point out that if he was worried about me losing my wood, then he should stop pumping booze into me, but I didn't want to be rude so I kept my mouth shut and swallowed. Maybe he knew about the meth, which makes you horny as fuck but kills erections dead on sight.

Scene 1:

Inquisitive pizza boy finds the door open. I nose in, sniffing for boy butt. Vince and Miguel are sprawled on the carpet, looking despondent over their homework. In a sleazy Brooklyn accent that sounds like my mouth is frozen, I offer to give them a lesson in adult male anatomy. The pizza took more than thirty minutes to get there, so they can have my pepperoni for free. That's the actual line I feed them. I'm serious. They take the pizza box and notice my growing erection. Vince gives me a noisy, wet blowjob with too many teeth. Trey walks in prissily and sits on the couch. I invite him to watch and wait his turn.

Scene 2:

Miguel and Vince trade rounds slurping my cock and foreskin. Miguel must have a thing for balls, because I can hardly have any screen time when he's not humming on them. The pizza gets cold, the homework gets forgotten, and I lose my hard-on because all this saliva reduces the friction I need to stay boned up. So much for Viagra. Trey's worked up a pathetic erection, a marker-sized tube hooked halfway up. His tongue's hanging out. I can't wait.

Scene 3:

Miguel is riding me emotively, but he's just embarrassing the both of us. Vince is watching and jerking off. I'm on my back, working on a fever that I'm sure the Viagra's given me, and I scan the vicinity for a bottle of Tylenol. Whitney Houston's "How Will I Know" is playing. Ted and JohnSilas are giving each other high-fives, pretending that things are going well, that they're taking their rightful place in the porn pantheon with Homework Hard-on 101. My dick goes soft again and slips out of Miguel's vacuous ass. It takes time for me to work it up again. The lube is the kind that gums up quickly and it keeps messing up the condom. There's a lot of waiting around. Vince chews on my nipple.

A burst of energy. I throw Miguel off me, scrunch Vince into the sofa, and pound his hole to the sound of his squeals. Miguel puts his head between my legs, and guess what? Gives me a hummer. Trey puts lip-gloss on and complains that he has to be somewhere. Ted tells him to "look alive or get off the set," so Trey sweeps my chest with a weak hand and lolls off into space.

Here are some myths about the making of porn films I'd like to clarify:

When a cock slides in all slippy, it's not the first time. It usually takes a few practice runs before it looks good enough for the cameras.

When two bodies are rocking, it doesn't necessarily mean that penetration is actually taking place.

Erect penises are precious and rare, and account for only a fraction of the time that the film is being shot.

No, the condom doesn't always come out clean.

No, the director doesn't get to fuck everybody in the room after the scenes wrap up.

No, there's no music.

And no, it's not sexy.

Scene 4:

I find out that this whole film is a vehicle for a sex move that Ted and JohnSilas mistakenly think they've invented. I'm ramming Vince's ass and thinking about Derek when Ted yells, "Helicopter!" which is my cue to make it happen. I pivot a hundred and eighty degrees on my cock and now I'm staring at the back of Vince's calves. The Velvet Mafia has struck again. The "new" move plays out pretty smoothly and I improvise a few variations. Miguel is watching us, his face a melted, post-coital smush. I bring his ass to my mouth like watermelon so he won't think I'm done with him. The lube tastes disgusting. More high-fives. I'm the only one in the room who knows that "the helicopter" is actually when you beat someone's face with your propeller, as coined by John Waters.

JohnSilas tells Trey to "put the fucking *People* magazine down, and at the very least, touch your dick and pretend you're watching."

Break:

Ted and JohnSilas take me aside. At first, I worry it has something to do with my immunity to Viagra.

"No, no, you're doing great," JohnSilas says.

"It's Trey," Ted honks through his nose cast. "What do we do with this kid?"

"I have an idea," I say, and immediately pop a boner so hard it hurts.

Scene 5:

I get Miguel and Vince to each hold one of Trey's chicken legs apart. I lose control of myself a little, seeing that pink hairless wound in his bum, knowing that my boozy breath is controlling his goose bumps. Now not even the Viagra can make me soft, not with me ramming one, then two, then three unlubed fingers up his ass and biting his bottom lip until it bleeds. He cries exactly like I expect him to, in blubbers that include the words "asshole," "cruel," "rapist," "police," and "why me." It's that last part that sets me off down a track of tunnel so dark that everything but his ass disappears. Peripheral vision, gone.

Why anybody?

I sink my dick into Trey's ass ever so slowly, giving him time to writhe as the pain sets in. I bury it to the hilt in a rectum I can feel isn't empty, at least not as far up his guts as my head is pushing. I swallow his silent scream with my mouth and loosen him up until he starts to kiss back. The way I set things up, the only way for him to fight is to come around. My cock is getting mucky with blood and shit, and I slide it all the way out so I can admire the residue of two facts: that he has never taken a dick so deep before, and that his enema was half-assed and useless to protect his insides from me. I go into a death spiral when I realize that I'm breaking him open. My cock is the kind that swells when it shoots and it forces Trey's eyes wide open. They focus somewhere behind me.

He cums into his own face.

End credits.

A burst of applause and the pop of Möet and Chandon, one of those giant magnums only a rich gay couple would buy. Ted and JohnSilas handed out rolls of hundreds and slow-danced with each other. Someone put on the Pet Shop Boys' "Opportunities (Let's Make Lots of Money)."

My Viagra fever had by then turned into this weird kind of ecstasy flush. I took my plastic champagne flute into the tanning bed and flipped the mauve lights on, hoping to decompress and stop shaking. I stuffed my cash into the dick sock so it wouldn't get burned, closed my eyes, and retreated to a place where people weren't constantly fucking each other in the presence of money. I had to imagine that I was alone.

Now, with Homework Hard-on 101 in my repertoire, I don't have to answer code 0020s or code 0099s anymore, and especially not code 0013s.

Maybe Derek was right. Maybe I *have* moved up in the food chain.

Having a sex life is a full-time job. I haven't written in forever. Between you and me, have I had the time?

It doesn't feel as bad as I thought it would. Yes, I had gone too far with Trey, but I could sense him conspiring with me to rewrite the boundaries of what was acceptable. If I hadn't felt him surrender his body to its own undoing, I might've held myself back, reconsidered my brutality, or pulled out altogether.

Just so you know.

A typical entrance. I walked into the loft and was greeted by Derek's back.

I figured that he was either painting or ignoring me. He had been acting distant lately, limiting his half of our conversations to a few perfunctory words, sometimes pretending I wasn't even there. He started to cook smaller and smaller meals until the leftovers I usually reheated disappeared altogether.

We'd worked out an unspoken agreement. He'd buy me anything I wanted, and I'd leave my latest story lying around somewhere for him to suck inspiration from. It had to have a young male protagonist experiencing some sort of beautiful agony. It had to be visceral and well written. I thought about buying him a stack of Dennis Cooper novels instead.

"Hey," I said.

No answer. Wink and Nod hadn't drawn in a while and had gone into semi-retirement. They smiled their ageless smiles at me, huddled against the outside walls of their TraceBox™, a structure they apparently couldn't bear to leave.

I heard a streaming sound, the sound of piss landing in a plastic bottle.

"You're just in time to see the birth of a new color, Booger. Now what would you call it?"

I peeked over his shoulder and squinted at the cloudy yellow.

"It looks like rancid honey."

He looked pleased by that, wrote it on a strip of masking tape, and labeled the half-quart Poland Spring water bottle.

"It's part of the collection. Go on, have a look at my latest before they go bad."

"What are you doing with these?"

"I've realized that there are colors, great ones, actually, that've yet to be invented. And I have every reason to believe that my kidneys are involved in this."

The brick wall under the factory windows had grown thick with piss-filled plastic bottles, each of them a slightly different tint of Derek. The color experiments were impressive:

amber molasses

lemongrass

oxidized copper

diluted tea

bruised spleen

chicken soup

nicotine ceiling

Sometimes when Derek left the apartment to go off on one of his art adventures, to scour the city for a color he knew had gone out of stock years ago, I would be left alone with his wall of piss. I'd scan these traces of him to analyze if he'd been eating properly, or drinking too much coffee, or getting enough iron.

On pathetic days, I'd try to match up a particular pissing to a particular day when we had argued, to see if the contents of his bladder could help me win the argument retroactively.

Other days, I'd hold the bottles up to the sunlight and look for answers to the tough questions:

Why was he so hard to reach after all this time? Why was he protecting the distance between us? Did jealousy actually run through him like poison when I told him about the guys I fucked for money? Where was this relationship going? What did we get from each other that we couldn't get on our own? Our relationship bred these questions prolifically.

In the bed that we would always magically end up in, like a fairy tale, I turned to Derek.

"What?" he said.

"Have you ever wondered why we don't have sex?"

Wink and Nod were silent, though I wanted them to make some noise right then, some bumps, anything.

"We don't have to," he said.

He kissed me on the forehead.

"Jaeven, I worry about you. You've been acting strange these days … Distant."

One afternoon, a bottle of murky pee gave me some insight: maybe only the purest relationships were able to survive without the element of sex.

I've seen unions defined by fucking, where marathon sessions were stand-in weddings, where torn condoms meant broken hearts. Maybe Derek and I have something pure enough to keep us floating above these body politics, immune to what sex can do to two people.

Or maybe I'm just crazy.

Our innocence is still frustrating. I can hardly stand his dry kisses, our hand-holding, our makeshift pajamas, but it's too late to replace this tenderness with desperate gropes in the dark.

The noise would destroy the silence, our bond.

"When you page me excessively," I say to Phil on the phone, "the massages become less and less inspired."

"I'm not calling for a massage. Congratulations."

"What for."

"Are you ready for this, Jaeven?"

"Yeah, what?"

"Word on the street is ... you're the new Boy New York."

I stare at the receiver.

"Well, fuck me," I say.

"You know that's not what we do," Phil says and hangs up.

Definition of a New York City hustler: A young man who undresses, looks pretty, and performs sexual favors for money. Typically callous, jaded, and rough around the edges. Torn jeans a plus. Not supposed to get affectionate, no matter how gooey he feels on the inside. Is usually available at all hours of the night but never before noon, leads a double life, and does whatever drugs his consorts want to see him do. Loathes other hustlers with unbounded passion.

He's paid $100-$700 (no tax) for a session from one to four hours, plus the following perks: anonymity, free taxi or limo service, free booze, free food, free drugs, and referrals.

A week in the life of one such professional, after being anointed Boy New York:

Monday

Wore Jack Nicholson sunglasses. Stopped by the Gem Spa newsstand to see which of my covers had come out. *Inches* was a keeper, especially with my head (hope it doesn't get too big) blocking out the N-C-H, and the caption "10 Inches of Monster Meat." The dangling cigarette made me look terminally sexy, but why did they have to exaggerate? I took twelve copies to autograph in clubs and make money with, but the guy at the cash only charged me for eleven, giving me that leering stare I've come to know. I signed his copy and bounced out.

Tuesday

Popped in on the Toilet Böys' webcast talk show to drool over Sean (meow). Phil was there, too, and he gave me some ridiculous leather duds to wear. He's so out of touch sometimes, thinking that people could see us on Internet radio. Sean grilled me about my body and it gave me a boner. I imagined him plowing my ass, churning me inside out and coating my guts with cum.

I was there to sign copies of the *Honcho* cover (hence the leather). They were auctioning them off to listeners who could answer questions about my life, and I got fancy by sticking a pen in my foreskin and autographing with my dick. One lucky winner of a signature was a guy who emailed in a description of what my shit looked like when I forgot to flush. Asshole. I think I know who it was, too.

Wednesday

Went to a magazine casting for *Blueboy*. This clearly had nothing to do with Phil, because he avoided these antiseptic California magazines like they were West Nile virus. Ridiculous tan lines, shaved chest and pits. The war on hair is a travesty of the human body, and it's what separates the East from the West.

This cheeseball Michael Lucas told me to take my clothes off and get hard. His Russian accent was so drippy, it had to be fake. He gave me three porn magazines to bone up to, all of which contained, incidentally, Michael Lucas oiled, naked, and giving soap opera faces. I left before His Smarminess could come back to check on me. I was not going to give him the satisfaction.

Thursday

Cruised into the New York premiere of Bruce LaBruce's bisexual opus Skin Gang at the ultra-trendy Performance Space 122. I was Phil's date for the night and laughed at all of his jokes, even when he forgot to make them funny.

Trey was there, looking jealous and giving us heat. At the urinals, he told me that one day he was going to be Boy New York and I'd be yesterday's used condom. "Whatever, jealous bitch," I said, then pissed on his leg.

Highlight of the film was when a hot skinhead jerked off while reading Hitler's Mein Kampf. LaBruce is such a genius. I respect subversive artists who focus on making you cum, but still manage to tick people off as a by-product. Some autograph hound asked me to sign a Homework Hard-on 101 box cover, but I just crumpled it and handed it back because I could tell the prick hadn't even seen the film.

Friday

Made a cameo appearance at the Forsythe and White Gallery in Chelsea. Aaron Cobbett played the social butterfly quite well, flitting among fans who came to see his photos of pouty muscle boys in color-saturated sets. His shots, according to HX magazine, "are making new again the concept of Lost Boy as objèt-trouvé, diamonds in the rough polished up with Vaseline."

In my photo, I was wearing a jock strap and enough pancake makeup to be a geisha girl. I made a few contacts (ahem) among admirers, raped the cheese platter of Roquefort, and skedaddled before Aaron got any funny ideas about shooting me again. On the way out, I bumped into his pornstar boyfriend Donnie Russo, who gave me a wink.

Saturday

Nothing. The way I like it. Watched Derek paint from my notebook.

When I went to bed, my eyes kept bouncing around and didn't want to close, so I went out into the empty city and tweaked around for interesting shit and ephemera:

Detached prescription lenses, shit-smeared newspaper (not a favorite), wish-bone halves, still-breathing fish heads dumped on the street in front of Chinatown restaurants (a favorite), plane tickets for two, dead birds throbbing with maggots, cum-filled condoms, lipstick tubes, baby strollers hanging from barbed wire, Coke bottles filled with piss, fake Fiorucci shoes (I can tell the difference, motherfuckers), peach pits sucked bald.

Objects, in case you haven't noticed, tell the parts of the story that people leave out.

Sunday

The Lord's day. Shot a video with Donnie Russo called *Brooklyn Meat Packers*. It was pretty hot pissing into this cute guy's mouth and wondering if he could taste the Red Bull and crystal meth. Getting artsy was the thing to do, ever since Terry Richardson had declared in *Nerve* magazine that the difference between art and porn had been erased forever. I had to play my part in the revolution, so I made a crude goblet with my foreskin for pigboy to sip from. Yikes, the looks he was giving me. I had to keep my left hand behind his head so he wouldn't slip a ring on it.

And that's a hustler's week in a New York minute.

Doormen with white gloves mean business.

At any residential building on the Upper East Side, they routinely chuck heads of state out by the scruff of their cheap Armani suits for the crime of not having an appointment.

But if you're a rent boy like me (funny how that expression doesn't seem to fit anymore), if you smell like sex and refer to tenants by their suite numbers, they'll lead you through the royal gates and apologize for having asked you any questions in the first place. I'm serious.

If you have a convenient hole in the thigh of your jeans, the doormen will know that you have business there, even if it's your first time. If they have any sense about them, they'll realize that your customers are the ones who give them a fat cash tip every Christmas.

The universe takes care if itself.

And you can't take any shit from them because they'll sniff out weakness and make you sign the guest register.

I walked into the elevator, a polished brass space capsule that was shiny and claustrophobic. The doorman followed me in. He hovered a finger over the elevator buttons and lifted his eyebrows, waiting for me to tell him what floor.

"How the hell should I know."

He nodded knowingly and pressed fourteen. His eyes. I could tell he'd been trained to use them to dilute embarrassment and make people feel better. Magnanimous prick.

"I'm going to fuck him," I told the doorman. "Let's just clear that up. Pick me up in half an hour."

I got out on the fourteenth (he knew better than to expect a tip from my ass) and found the suite door open. I walked into a princess palace of white carpeting and kitschy crystal figurines, shelves crammed with priceless pieces of junk, and antique Chinese furniture sagging under sick wastes of money. Only the stacks of manuscripts seemed out of place.

"You must be the famous Jaeven. I'm Dennis."

I gave him fifty-three, fifty-four, the type of daddy who took care of his boy. I gave my crotch a squeeze and made sure he saw it.

"Yeah. Vodka cranberry."

"You're good at this. Ice?"

"Why not."

"Take your shoes off," he said.

"How do I know you're not going to steal them?"

A butler in a tuxedo (who I guess had been listening) served my drink on a mother-of-pearl tray—without meeting my eyes, of course.

The lights of New York City pulled me like tractor beams to the big bay window and I stood there transfixed, wondering how long I would own all this, how long my reign as Boy New York would last. Dennis reached over my shoulder and laid a stash of twenties in my hand.

I didn't need to look to know that they were twenties. I can distinguish the smell of a twenty from a hundred from a single. They have different degrees of dirt on them. They're born of different transactions. Hundreds have this sinister scent about them, because the more zeroes you tack on, the higher the stakes. They usually smell like puke, for some reason. Twenties smell like booze. Tens and fives smell alternately like crotch and ass, and that's why I can never tell them apart.

The only thing I wasn't sure about was whether or not he included a tip. I wasn't about to count the money, because only debutantes do that.

I folded the bills into my pocket, the hustler signal that it's a go. In any other part of town, he would've put the money on the nightstand and we'd both stare at it until the transaction was complete. This was the Upper East Side, however, and we both knew the rules were different.

After the Fire's "Der Kommissar" ran through my head. *Don't turn around.* Because if you do, he's going to kiss you. These old men, in the end, want affection more than anything else.

You can never be sure, though. And things can get dangerous in soundproof buildings where you have to rely on doormen to let you out.

We went to the bedroom and I sat on the bed, waiting for him to make me shuck my pants. Instead, he pulled up a chair in front of me.

"Take off your socks, one at a time."

So I ripped one off and dropped it on the carpet. He looked disappointed.

"Who sent you here, anyways?"

"Phil McDougall."

"Didn't he tell you anything about me? That I'm specific?"

I was confused so I asked for another drink. The butler brought it, left, and locked the door behind him. Dennis looked at me and wiped the sweat off his brow with a handkerchief.

"I need you to do it s-l-o-w-l-y. Is that too difficult?"

"No, sure."

"Okay, now continue."

He knelt like a shoe salesman.

I slinked the other sock off slowly, like a condom I'd just blown a load into. It was weird but I was getting into it. I'd never thought the curly hairs around my ankle were sexy until now, until they were feeding someone's desire through anticipation and deprivation. He was sweating contentedly a few feet away, happy to be without the object he wanted most in the world: my sock.

Now this was power, I thought. If only I could wield it in the other parts of my life.

The sock was halfway off my foot when the funk started to waft up—me in all my raunchy glory. He was trying his best not to sniff, and I could see in his face that holding back was getting him off. Just thinking about how I had a human puppet more than twice my age made my dick pudge out and poke through the hole in my jeans. My erection didn't interest him in the least.

"Now take it off completely."

"Slowly?"

"What do you think?"

So I did as he said, exposing dirty toenails, cracked and misshapen. I handed him the sock and he brought it up to his nose with both hands like it contained the last breath of oxygen in outer space. As he inhaled my funk for a solid minute (I shit you not), he turned away from me and gazed out the window at the twinkling lights of New York City.

He was gone.

Eyes tearing up, shirt drenched with sweat. It wasn't my place to know why, even if I was the angel making it happen. It wasn't about me anymore. I was witnessing a religious experience. It was intestinal.

It doesn't mean I was used to feeling ignored in these situations.

I put my shoes on and the butler let me out. The doorman was waiting in the elevator to take me down and I pretended he wasn't there. I walked out into the night, wondering where I was supposed to find a matching sock before going dancing at Jackie 60.

The sock fucker didn't tip me.

I get pissed off when wealthy Manhattanites don't tip, because the people around them have to pretend that everything happens by itself.

Valets have to pretend that cars park themselves, and security guards have to pretend that no unwanted guests ever try to sneak into the building.

I don't hate doormen as much as you think I do.

They have it the hardest because they have to pretend that their building is immune to ice and snow in the winter. They also have to pretend that doors open by themselves, that clothes dry-clean themselves, that taxis hail themselves, that FedEx packages float up the stairs by themselves, that garbage bags are transported magically to the dumpster courtesy of fairy dust from Bloomingdale's. They're also dealers in kink, and masters of covering trails and keeping secrets. When you don't see the doorman in the lobby, it's because he's manning the back door.

It sticks in my craw that there's a whole network of underlings, me included, who are expected to conspire together to make sure that the world runs smoothly and that everything happens with the utmost discretion—for nothing more than the going rate.

Our charge is heavy, but a tip would somehow make it alright.

I sent out a new short story to eleven literary magazines today.

Here's how it went down.

I was getting sick of two-faced editors who demand exclusive submissions but are quite content to reject the unpublished, hundreds at a time. Does that make sense? I decided to start playing by my own rules. I spent hours in Barnes and Noble, nosing out which magazines felt empty without my writing. Multiple submissions it was.

Since I don't believe in karma—a philosophy that says I deserve the life I've had—the worst that could happen would be to get two acceptance letters for the same story.

I'm doing my best to stay positive, but I have to tell you that trying to get published (a word I've grown to hate) feels like buying raffle tickets for a prize that's already been given out by a church that's already burned down. Eventually, you're going to stop trying.

Summer's starting to fizzle out and the nights are getting cool. There are only a couple of months left in 1999 for me to make my mark in the world of writing, before the millennium sweeps in and changes things forever. I don't want to think of what January 1 will be like if I'm in the same place I was the last time that date rolled around: a writer with no readers.

Writing guides and the crappy advice they give don't work, so I don't buy or steal them anymore. This latest story comes from inside me. I threw myself into it and laced it with venom. It's probably the most mature thing I've written so far, and I think it reads reasonably well.

The story.

The kid wasn't adapting well to reform school. He was an outcast from the moment he got there, but it was all for the better. If he was going to survive a place like that, he needed the resourcefulness of a lone wolf.

The school designed lessons to destroy his soul, one wisp at a time.

In Morals class, they taught him about the importance of family. He sat through slideshows of mother, father, daughter, son, image after image of the same perfect unit, but with different actors every time. They said that the family was the institution that kept the world from falling apart. It was the epicenter of nurturing love, and the foundation that held up the pillars of society. The kid noticed that none of the slides depicted his own family.

In Morals class, they taught him that people "reap what they sow," that people get what they deserve, that those who reject their family don't deserve to have one.

They taught him that murderers go to prison and the lazy get sentenced to the street.

In Morals class, the kid learned that America was a Christian country because even the outcasts were given a second chance.

The only moments when the kid could be himself—when he wasn't being brainwashed with ideas that gradually, against his will, started to seep in and make sense—was when he was in the bathroom. His wolfishness took over. He discovered ways of angling himself at a urinal to arouse the curiosity of younger boys. Perhaps they missed their older brothers, or had never seen something so dark and wrinkly take a piss.

In Morals class, they never said anything about the body and how it was supposed to grow and feel. With wolfish style, the kid was able to teach the boys all they needed to know about feeling good. He awakened them. A young body awakens gracefully like a grenade, like a tiny match flame in a room filled with propane gas.

The kid was thrown out of reform school. His family wouldn't take him back, so he wound up on the street, where the real wolves got hold of him. They ripped him apart but the kid didn't lose hope, knowing that living in a Christian country, he would eventually be given a second chance.

Allow me to make some predictions about the end of the world:

At 12:00 a.m. EST on January 1, 2000, slot machines at a racetrack in Delaware will stop working as a result of the Y2K millennium bug. Approximately 150 slots will fizzle, causing panic among gamblers who'll claim that they were between five and ten quarters away from winning. Slot fiends from around the world will clamor to play these "unlucky" machines, creating a two-year waiting list.

If the world still exists, of course.

My latest food chain demotion was a trick at Broadway and twenty-third, a sex pig from Brazil who worked as a UN caterer. We did crystal together and he asked me to fuck him without a condom. He paid me first.

Like everything else, I said why not.

It's not that I didn't know it was dangerous, but I do plenty of other things that are just as dangerous. I stick my bare hands down garbage cans and hope nothing pricks me. I sleep standing on subway platforms, tottering at the edge. I suck cock in dim lighting and forget to bring my genital warts questionnaire. The point I'm making is that if you have one exception in your risk management system, it all breaks down. There's also something about the millennium that's making me care less and less about the things that are supposed to matter.

When I came in his gaping ass, he gave me a satisfied look over his shoulder, a look that said his life was now full and complete with my sperm swimming up into him.

We squatted on the floor, watching the sun rise over an unchangeable skyline, rubbing our sofa-creased kneecaps. Between cigarettes, I scarfed whatever he had in the mini-fridge, chewing and smoking as meaningfully as I thought I should after having unprotected sex.

At first there was small talk. I explained how my life was slowly going down the shitter. He told me about UN toga parties where diplomats got unhinged and drank champagne up the ass. I had the nagging feeling this wasn't the first time he'd barebacked, then by the third cigarette, the nag had grown into a suspicion that ate up conversation like a black hole. I felt really stupid.

"You should go get an HIV test," he said.

"Yeah, why not," I said.

Like everything else.

I try to ignore how hustling steals little pieces of your body and scatters them all over the city, and how you have to summon every last bit of energy to rematerialize into something whole again.

When you're flying by the seat of your bankable ass from photo shoot to photo shoot, it won't occur to you that you're a prostitute.

When you step out of a limo with a glass of champagne, and a bodyguard escorts you through a tweaked-up crowd, past the velvet rope, and into Manhattan's hottest night box, it doesn't occur to you that you're anything other than a celebrity.

When your likeness is enshrined on a gallery wall and the New York Times posits aesthetic arguments about your body, it doesn't occur to you that you're incidental, nevermind disposable.

The problem with prostitution is that no matter how high up in the food chain you get, there's no such thing as an upgrade. It's always prostitution, so long as your employer knows how desperate you are for cash.

The truth of whoredom only sinks in when someone pays you by shoving bills into your mouth. When they think a grubby, crumpled-up hundred gives them the right to push you around, slap you, choke you, spit in your face, burn you with cigarettes, punch black eyes into you, fuck you till you bleed, cum in your eye, and piss in your wounds. When they make you lick your own shit off their middle finger.

But the truth of whoredom only *really* sets in when someone finds it unimaginable, inconceivable, and preposterous that you might have anything to write about other than the best way to get dried lube out of your hair.

When your intelligence becomes a running gag.

When you become subhuman.

It dry-fucks the soul something bad.

Dear Mr Marshall,

Although your submission doesn't fit our current publishing needs, we thank you for submitting your story. We have noted that the New York Times recently covered a photography exhibit in which you participated. We encourage you to put as much passion into your fiction as you do into modeling.

The editors wish you the best in whatever career you choose, or whatever career chooses you.

Sincerely,

New York Times Magazine

A gay couple I know, Karanvir and Michael, asked me to move with them to a geodesic dome in the Arizona desert, one they had bought to prepare for the coming Y2K meltdown. They had maxed out eight credit cards between them. I refused, wished them good luck with the greenhouse farming and the life of debt, and told them never to call me again.

I was going to watch the world fizzle and burn from the best vantage point: Times Square.

≡

"What are you writing today?" Richard asked.

Snap, click, whirr.

"Personal stuff."

"Of course, but hello? Try me."

"It's about Derek."

He looked at me through a lens I can now almost see myself through.

"Don't tell me you're falling in love."

Click.

"Well, no, but ... we're together. And I'm learning things about myself."

"And you're saying it's all because of him?"

"No, but he's involved."

"In what?"

"My changes."

"Right, so you're writing about yourself then, not about him."

"I guess."

"By the way, I'm asking you, not telling you."

"I know."

Richard's wise. I'm not sure what such a guru gets out of taking pictures of a hustler scribbling shirtless on his floor, though I'm sure he'll eventually fill me in.

He's wise, but I don't think he sees the whole picture.

Shit and ephemera from another one of my tweak runs:

Japanese transvestite manga porn, razors, poetry, socks, roses, brand new televisions, vomit broken down into ingredients, unlabeled keys dangling over sewers, dead bumblebees, anonymous phone numbers on scraps of paper, unidentifiable plastic widgets.

Traces of a New York that one day, in all likelihood, won't exist.

Beauty is designed to crumble just when you learn to appreciate it.

≣

Pretend Indian massage and bullshit chakra-tuning to Spandau Ballet's "True," so good it can be done with or without clothes.

Playguy cover and special pin-up centerfold, September 1999. Crystal Vase shoots in a well-known but secret midtown BDSM dungeon. It's a duo set, and I'm wearing an eye patch. I lay a sales boy from the Body Shop on a hospital gurney and make him drink my cum. He gives good camera winces when I pretend to tattoo my name into his arm with a cigarette. I make sure to pause and smile for Crystal.

Fan letter to *Playguy*, October 1999:

> Dear *Playguy*,
> What a hottie! Let me know where you found him, so I can snap up the next one before your photographers do. Please tell Trey that he can come play volleyball on my property anytime, though I don't trust myself not to chain him to

the net. Lord knows what I'd do with that belly button and those candy lips. Yum! It's nice to see such a fresh face on my nightstand, and I owe it all to *Playguy*. Thanks, guys.

I do have one bone to pick, however (no pun intended). It seems as if I've seen your model Jaeven a few too many times this year. He's still kind of hot, but the j/o fantasies are getting kind of old. And what happened to his teeth? Time to bring in the new crop, don't you think? Otherwise, great job with the magazine. Keep up the good work.
Harry in Great Falls, Missouri

Hello,
No. Good luck and please submit again.
Sincerely,
Tin House

"I believe in your work," Derek tells me in bed.

I don't say anything.

"Can I ask you a question?" he says, stroking my face. "Why doesn't the kid in your stories have a name?"

I don't say anything because I know that as soon as I open my mouth, I'll just end up crying a year's worth of shit that he won't be able to decipher.

Vespers that bloom in the dark, trashed artwork, torn manuscripts, poetry you'll never see, last words spoken to dying people who are actually already dead, most definitions of love, most definitions of death, things that are supposed to happen but don't.

Part 3

BECAUSE CENTRAL PARK LOOKS freaky when all the leaves fall off and the trees just stand there naked and cold. Because naked bodies are hiding under heavier and heavier clothes.

My fingers are starting to freeze again when I smoke, and the air is starting to smoke when I breathe.

The cold rain can throw me into such a wicked mood.

"Jaeven Marshall, are you listening to me?"

Derek Brathwaite towered over my chair like a police investigator, an unlikely detective in his paint-smeared shirt. He was staring at me, and maybe through me a little.

"What does it look like," I said.

"Of course you're listening. You're a speed freak. You have no choice but to be attentive."

"I need to be aware of my surroundings."

"You chew your lips off."

"I need meth for my ADD. You know I'd be a wreck without it."

"You're doing it right now."

"That's because you're sketching me out!"

"Shut up and listen to me. I've been taking notes on you."

He reached into his pocket and pulled out a sheet of loose leaf, my life laid out in point form. I started to twirl a cowlick near the crown of my head.

"Insomnia."

"So what?"

"I don't know you anymore. You kick the turtles half the time, you're so out of it."

"I turn most of my tricks at night."

"Newsflash, Jaeven. They don't page you anymore, and now you're blowing all of my money on meth."

"Oh, so now it's *your* money. Mommy cut you off?"

"Don't be cute, sugar-pie, it doesn't suit you. When was your last trick, and how long did that money last?"

"Whatever."

My devil horn took shape under my working fingers.

"Have you looked at your teeth in a mirror lately? You have meth mouth. It's repulsive."

"Have you offered to pay for a dentist?" I zinged back.

"Don't blame this on me. You're the one who's fucked up."

He crinkled the paper, I'm guessing to signal a little victory.

"Dehydration, nausea, diarrhea, loss of appetite, rapid heartbeat, acne."

"You got that list out of a book. Do you see any acne?"

"You're acting defensive because I'm confronting you. That's another sign."

"Wouldn't you defend yourself against false accusations? I don't have acne and I don't shit my pants ... Jeeeez. Did you learn all this from some talk show or something? One of those shows where everything wrong that happens is *because* of something? They tell you to confront the person, but they don't tell you that it only brings more conflict into the relationship. Well, *guess what*—messed-up shit happens all the time, so you'd better get used to it. And I never, ever tweak in front of you."

"Talkativeness."

"Fuck off."

The cowlick. I was losing this.

"And please, stop punding. I can't take it."

He sighed, walked over to the wall, and studied his latest canvas. My latest unpublished short story. A reform school never looked so piss-colored.

What's punding?" I said.

"Compulsive fascination with repetitive tasks. The twirling, the chewing your lips, the grinding your jaw, the trash you bring home— it's driving me mental."

I was about to blurt out that life was nothing but a compulsive fascination with repetitive tasks, that we're all just doing the same old thing because we're afraid to try something new, that it's the punding that keeps us too busy to kill ourselves or to hurt others too much, but I took a different tack instead, one I instantly regretted.

"Why are you doing this? Why are we having this conversation?"

I don't know. I was expecting him to say that it was because he was worried about me, that he cared about me, that he wanted us to have a fresh start. But it was something very different.

"Because that's how you talk to liars." He folded the sheet of paper back into his pocket and looked me in the eye. "You never told me the cops busted you for possession."

"They dropped the charges. I'm not technically a criminal."

"No, but you're a liar."

"I just forgot to tell you."

"That's still lying."

I can feel the itch of things to come:

At 12:00 a.m. EST on January 1, 2000, Kurt Vonnegut's personal computer will list the date as being 19100, eerily reminiscent of the "timequakes" that so many of his novels have foretold. The author will then start working on a new novel of "suggested corrections" to the chronology of his previous ones, since his science-fiction hypotheses were based on the assumption that a "timequake" would never actually occur. Mr Vonnegut will leave the Y2K glitch on his personal computer unfixed, and he'll continue to live 17,100 years in the future.

Wanna bet?

Dear Writer,

We suggest that you take a writing course, and/or read the following books published by our parent company: *The UnFrustrated Writer*, and *Avoiding the Draft*.

Thank you for considering us, but please refrain from submitting again.

Sincerely,

The Believer

"Did that really happen?" Richard asks, reading a random page over my shoulder.

Click, snap, refocus.

"That's not the point."

"Right, yeah, I get it."

Zoom.

"Did the United States stop importing jasmine tea?" I say, tapping the empty cup with my pen.

New York got its first snowfall of the season last night. At first, it looked like the kind of snow the city's underground heat would melt, but it stuck around and piled up. It's funny watching bike messengers wobble through the mini-drifts gathered at the curb.

Jackie 60 dress code, Valerie Solanas Tribute Night—We Can All Shoot Andy Warhol:

Pop art razor blades, Boho dykewear, Hobo dykewear, newsboy caps, geo-patterned Diane von Furstenberg hip holsters, Factory ammo belts, Nico eyeliner, sixties hair, typewriter ribbon, street urchin fatigues with utility pockets, powdered white wigs, bulletproof vests, fake blood, Andy Warhol silkscreens on Stephen Sprouse knockoffs, flash boxes, Super-8 wind-up cameras, sewer scum.

Yesterday was December 8, the day I turned twenty-three.

Whoopty-freaking-doo.

I decided to go out and have some fun, to try and forget that I also had twenty-three days left to turn this year around and prevent it from being a complete failure.

Jackie 60 was full of night crawlers and Factory wannabes all trying to make out with each other. Morrissey was warbling through a remix of The Smiths' "There Is a Light That Never Goes Out," a song I know all too well. I don't know why DJ Johnny Dynell thought the song had anything to do with Andy Warhol, but he's earned enough cred to be given the benefit of the doubt.

The itch got to me, so I made a batch of Red Bull and crystal, probably one of my last. Then I finessed a couple of drinks out of some thirty-something easy marks.

I saw him canted against a wall watching the dancers—the same goth boy who was making eyes with me the last time I had come to Jackie 60. He was dressed in a black Elvis Costello suit and tie as if he were going to a funeral, or a wedding, or maybe that's just how he woke up. I was in love with his canvas sneakers. He was so my speed.

I crept up behind him and he noticed right away. There was a flash in his eyes and a lull in the music. God bless Dynell for misplacing his wax.

"Let's go to your place," I said.

"Right."

We didn't say much, walking on the deserted sidewalk through Chelsea, kicking through the snow. It was too cold to smoke, so I hid my hands in my sleeves. He told me his name was Adam.

I followed him into a sketchy-looking establishment on Fourteenth Street.

"This is it," he said.

A central L-shaped hallway branched off into different rooms, divided by wonky sheets of drywall covered in colorful graffiti tags and phone numbers of people who suck cock.

"This is *what*." I said.

"The Gavin Brown Gallery. My place. It's an art installation, and I'm validating it by living here."

"I get it," I said, though I didn't get it at all.

It's weird, what keeps your legs from running when your brain says go. I felt guilty just being there, like I was cheating on Derek. It made no sense, but feelings can be so blind to logic.

Adam must have noticed my hesitation. He planted his mouth over mine for a solid minute. His spit was more viscous than mine, and it felt warm and silky on my tongue. His eyes, lined with black kohl, were closed, and I wondered what pictures he was playing on the inside of his head to have melted his sullenness into this living liquid in my mouth. I could taste traces of sadness in him, but more than that. Lightlessness.

A different kind of logic took hold of me. Why should I feel guilty about having sex, for the first time I can remember, with someone I'm attracted to?

"Where's the bedroom," I said.

"Pick one."

I pushed him backwards into the nearest corner and peeled his shirt over his head. His chest was white and fragile, almost bird-like, with two nipple piercings that looked slightly raw and infected. I left my clothes on because I wasn't in the mood to be vulnerable—not just yet.

I shucked his pants for him and bent him over. Adam's crack was filled with this soft, mousy brown fur that curled into a cowlick near his tailbone when I made it wet with a lascivious lick.

"I think it's really sexy that you wear sneakers with a suit," I said, ruining the wordless state of bliss that we had achieved.

I buried my face in his bum and he squirmed. I licked circles around his hole and then pushed my tongue into him. He tasted like apples and sweat, almost bittersweet. When he moaned, I could feel the vibrations buzz right through my mouth. I don't think I've ever felt more intimate with anybody, save Derek. There was something exotic about eating out a queer goth boy's butt. Something dark.

God freeze this minute forever. I was getting weepy. Who said you had to take your clothes off to be vulnerable?

Adam turned his head and looked at me over his shoulder.

"I want you to fuck me until I lose my voice screaming your name."

I told him what it was, and exactly how to pronounce it.

I left much later, when the sun began to spill into this corner of the city, when Adam was sleeping and voiceless, and when missing Derek hurt too much.

≋

This is how I experience Richard in traces:

When I pass a car window and see my reflection, when I feel beautiful despite a lip ring infection or a rash-du-jour or a nose-diving sense of self-worth, when I'm tempted to spread my ass cheeks and then realize I have other things to offer, when I'm tying my shoes, when I find myself retelling a part of my journey, when I feel vulnerable.

It would be easier to find shit and ephemera with a MetroCard bent to work forever. Nevertheless, the city gives up its dead:

Revolvers, shell casings, kitchen knives, pacifiers, photo albums with pages torn out, fingerless gloves that smell like perfume, rolled-up panties that smell like pussy, half-full bottles of Absolut vodka, bones, baby dolls with holes cut into their crotches.

Could these lists be what Derek means by "punding"?

When I walked into the loft, Derek was bent over the table arranging a bunch of crocuses and hydrangea. He was wearing a dress-shirt buttoned up to the top and his blond bangs were combed gorgeously. There were two art deco ceramic plates on the table, each of them rimmed with steaming white asparagus shoots under melting butter, a pork chop, and a frumpy mound of mashed potatoes.

I was missing something.

"Good morning and happy birthday," he said. "I figured I'd just reheat your birthday dinner ... you don't mind having asparagus for breakfast, do you?"

I just stood there.

"What was his name?"

"Adam," I said morosely, aware of his tactics.

"Enjoy fucking him?"

"Please, just not today. Let's not fight."

"Of course. The sex tired you out."

"Listen, I'm sorry."

"Don't apologize. It's a free country."

We sat down and started on my birthday breakfast. Derek uncorked a bottle of 1988 Château Margaux red that I know he'd been saving for a special occasion. He poured himself a glass and took a swig, looking out the window, his smarmy smile slowly dissolving. My glass was still empty.

"I'm sorry for missing dinner," I said.

"If you don't cut down on the fucking meth, you'll have to move out, unless I have the energy to check you in—you know where. I can't live with an addict."

"Just give me some time," I said. "I can do it."

Thank you for sending your story, but *Ploughshares* is closed to submissions until further notice.

Please be assured that it has nothing to do with the quality of your writing.

The Editors

The thought *has* crossed my mind, by the way, to submit these rejection letters. Some of them are real pieces of work.

Jackie 60 dress code, Y2K Madness, December 28, 1999:

End-of-the-world mood rings, binary code safety vests, glow-in-the-dark underwear, steel-toe John Fluevog shitkickers, *Tron* helmets with spelunker headlamps, Armageddon body armor, millennial nudism, clit rings and other Raelian homing devices, "R.I.P. Microsoft" pin-back buttons, *Strange Days* simulated reality brain SQUIDs, cyberpunk gear, gold bullion Hermes belt buckles.

Too bad I wasn't there.

There were only two days left in 1999.

It was coming down to last chances.

My publishing strategy—mail and wait, wait, wait—wasn't aggressive enough to catch anyone's attention. I've learned that you have to fight for what you want. Nobody's going to give it to you otherwise. I had to meet a powerful person, like I had done to become Boy New York, and convince them I was "the one."

I had to get a literary agent.

The brass revolving doors swept me into the highfalutin lobby of the Fifth Avenue tower. You know, an indoor waterfall and a general overdose on feng shui. I adjusted my skinny tie and sport jacket, feeling more like Tom Hadley in a Spandau Ballet video than a writer.

It hadn't been easy to get an appointment with a Gray and Brennan literary agent because the secretaries there hang up as soon as you mention the plague word "unpublished." I had to call back a few times with a less poisoned pitch.

I got off the elevator on the fourteenth floor. That number, for some reason, gave me a wave of body anxiety.

The on-duty secretary was a mincing twink dressed in Old Navy.

"Name."

"Jaeven Marshall. I'm here to see Mr Brennan."

"You and ten thousand other people."

"Yeah, well, I have an appointment. Do your job and look it up."

He smiled a "fuck you" at me, and made the call.

Mr Brennan walked in.

Holy Angels of nipple torture.

His shock cancelled mine out and we shook hands uncomfortably. I glanced at my hand after he let go, expecting to find a wad of cash, a reflex I can't seem to lose.

Dennis the sock freak was looking much different in his Armani suit.

My worlds collide all the fucking time.

"Come to my office."

I followed him and he closed the door carefully and meticulously, turning the brass handle so it wouldn't make noise.

"What the hell are you doing here? We can't do this at work. How did you—"

"I'm here to show you my writing."

"Funny, ha-ha. Now get serious. This is unethical of you as a businessperson," he said.

"No, look, I brought my stories."

I handed him my notebook. I could've given him the copies that I'd printed for submission, but I wanted him to see the material in its natural habitat. The writing was pretty neat, so I didn't think it was a major deal that it was in pencil and sometimes ran upside-down and even off the page. He held my coffee-stained masterpiece up to the light and squinted a face full of crow's feet at it. My blood work. A year of personal excavation.

"This is a fucking diary. Are you kidding me?"

He handed it back and looked at me matter-of-factly.

"I can't do anything with this."

He was hoping I would go away, the asshole. Little did he know that he was my gift horse, and that I was going to ride his aging ass to the glue factory.

"You know," I said, taking liberties to pick up and spit-shine a 1986 World Series baseball signed by the Mets, "we find ourselves in a bit of a situation here."

I motioned to the door with my head.

"Gray and Brennan."

Balls in hand. I knew where he worked.

"What do you want?" Dennis said.

"I want to get published."

"I can't ... we can't do that. It's not going to happen."

"Why not?"

He gave me a vicious smile.

"Because writers are writers and whores are whores."

He opened a desk drawer and flipped me a dog bone of twenties rolled together with rubber bands (I didn't have to give him a sock this time), along with a fat Ziploc baggie of meth. The crystals refracted the light right through my skull. I could already feel the high coming on, choking down the guilt and images of a furious Derek.

"That's hard to get," I told him.

"Best of luck placing your work," he said. "We don't know each other."

"How did it go today?"

I wanted to have good news for him.

"It was whatever."

Wink and Nod, now permanently retired to a life of daffodils and hydroponic lettuce, bumped affectionately into my shins.

Derek walked me over to the far wall of the loft.

"I'm showing these tomorrow."

He gestured to a dozen canvases in front of us.

"You're having your first show?" I said. "Why didn't you tell me?"

"I wanted it to be a surprise."

The paintings were truly beautiful, and I'm not just saying that to be supportive. The profusion of color left me breathless. It was overwhelming to see my stories told through his brushstrokes. I saw all of his moods washing into each other, out of each other, changing with the ebb and flow of his half of our relationship.

It made sense, in a circular kind of way, that these paintings were inspired by my stories and failures. Derek had rescued me from the spits and kicks of the street, then he gave me a brand new start, created a safe space for me to incubate in, and watched over me as I grew. I owed him everything. Being a good muse was the least I could do.

"What do you think?" he said.

"You're beautiful."

I kissed him. His eyebrows floated in surprise.

"It's at the Forsythe and White Gallery," he said. "The show starts at midnight, January 1, so don't be late. You should come a little early."

"I will."

"Are you ... are you okay with me selling these paintings? I mean ..."

I could have felt violated. I could have acted jealous. There were so many petty ways I could have quashed his painting career, but seeing him happy felt too damn good.

"It's fine. Just make sure you charge more than I do."

Shit's way more wonky than I could've imagined:

Maine's Department of Motor Vehicles sent ownership titles for "horseless carriages" to buyers of year 2000 cars and trucks. The vehicle registry system was in a tizzy and misread 2000 as 1900. Less than half of the 800 car owners and 1,400 truck owners who found out they were driving buggies asked the DMV for new titles.

"Jaeven," Derek said in bed that night.

"I've been taking less," I said. "It feels weird, but I've been cutting down."

That's what I told him. You can probably figure out the truth.

Sleep? Who can sleep on a night like this? I checked the mailbox one last time.

As if.

It's the middle of the night and I'm in the bathroom, holding my new Ziploc of meth. There's a toilet, a sink, and a shower drain, so I'd have no excuse not to dissolve this habit once and for all if I wanted to, unless to spare innocent sewer rats from a wicked tweak high.

There's something I'd like to bring up, here in the bathroom in the middle of the night. Derek is blaming our relationship troubles exclusively on meth, which is unfair and delusional. There were countless times when we iced each other, pushed buttons, and hid the truth, and that had nothing to do with drugs. Even you know that.

And anyways, you're supposed to quit for yourself, not for anyone else.

Millennial madness. The last night of the last thousand years.

The rumor was that you couldn't find a cop for miles because they were all in Times Square preparing for the end of civilization.

The rumor was that if you were in a space shuttle at the moment the ball dropped and the clock struck twelve, all you'd see was our crazy island fading to red and blue—police cruiser light.

The rumor was that the cops were going to ruin this party something bad.

I went to Coyote Ugly to get into the Y2K spirit before going to Derek's show. Phil was buying drinks and I got a little wonky, dancing to Madness's "Our House." I ended up sprawled on a table of Windex shooters, licking myself clean. Chase was there, schmoozing up whoever he could before Y2K shut his career down. Mine had already dried up, along with the batteries in my pager.

Peter Jennings was rapping on ABC's *New Year's Eve Special* on the TV above the bar:

"Humanity has reached a crossroads tonight, the end of a millennium and the start of a new one. John F. Kennedy once said, 'the only thing to fear is fear itself.'"

Jennings should've been quoting *The Far Side*, not Kennedy. Just because.

"There's nothing else to do but wait. We have a Y2K specialist here in the studio to tell us what the likelihood is of losing the national power grid ..."

The camera fell off his face and onto the floor. The grip must've dropped it to get his drunk on, realizing that in a few hours, he wouldn't need that crappy job of framing Jennings' pretty head anymore.

According to the Y2K "specialist," bank machines would be spitting out hundred-dollar bills at the end of the world.

Head starts were all the rage. People had been lining up at Chase Manhattan ATMs for a good week. There were runs on food, water, batteries, radios, Cheetos, candles, duct tape, hypodermic needles, ammo, firearms, bullets, rifles, 38's and 45's, cross-bows, arrows, pepper-spray, vodka, beer, cash, gold, stocks and bonds, generators, oxygen tanks, chemical weapon antidotes, vaccines, three-ply Charmin toilet paper, underwear, DVDs, PlayStation video games, and gasoline.

There's a fine line between emergency preparedness and hysteria fuelled by clever marketing.

It was around this point that reality hazed out on me. I may have been there in the bar, I may have been outside skimming for priceless trash, and I may have been back home, far away from New York City. The feeling was scary but fun.

I seemed to be dancing with some guy wearing a Nike tracksuit, chunky gold jewelry, and a pair of neon fly glasses that covered half his face.

"You're cute," he said to me. "What do you do?"

"I'm a pornstar."

"Must be a fun job."

"I get to shake my dick at people. It's not bad. What are you supposed to be, a deejay or something?"

"Not exactly."

"It's okay. I like deejays."

Then a drag mama in a bad wig bumped into me and stuck her mouth in my ear.

"Don't you know who that is?" she said.

"He's probably one of my fans. What difference does it make which one?"

I took fly guy's cocktail, downed it, and fondled the chain clunking around his neck. He smirked.

"I'm a writer, too," I told him. "It's just that I'm naked sometimes."

"Then I might have a job for you," he said, laughing.

I was supposed to say something.

That's when I recognized him, or at least who I imagined was in front of me.

I was now supposed to say something to David fucking LaChurch. What were the chances? Another drink of indeterminate composition helped keep my mind from shattering too violently. This was the writing opportunity of a lifetime. Was he going to ask me to work on his film?

Peter Jennings had given up on being decorous, and instead, was playing crazy eights with his co-anchors, looking bedroom sexy without a tie. Even he had figured out that it was all coming to an end. The sound cut out (probably another technician gone to the ATM) and was replaced by The Talking Heads' "Road to Nowhere."

"We're leaving, but you should come with," David said. "The limo's taking us to Windows on the World."

His posse piled into the limo. I was squinched in with his family of beautiful freaks and unlikely superstars. Bonnie Le Hoar, transsexual of the gods, was nearly suffocating me with silicone tits covered only by silver tassels. If you don't know what she looks like, picture Marilyn Monroe's face stung by a swarm of bees. Angry ones that have a thing for lips.

Plastic surgery nightmare Kitty Braunstein was purring beside her. She gave me this shell-shocked stare and hissed. If you don't know what she looks like, picture a mountain lion with chin and cheek implants swollen with collagen and beaten with a baseball bat.

This was one sweet dream.

Möet and Chandon all around, and the limo drove off.

Now, if you know these two, you know they're best friends, which means they love to fight. You could just feel it coming. Let's imagine that Bonnie was going on about the Time Tranny watch that Swatch had just released with her face on it, designed by David LaChurch. She was so fabulous, yada yada yada. Kitty's botox pout was getting more and more pronounced. She had to say something, or that lower lip was going to explode.

"My greyhound's water bowl is worth more than that stupid watch," Kitty said in her Swiss accent of diamonds and gravel.

"Don't be jealous, honey," Bonnie retorted. "We'll get you a water bowl."

"Bitch."

"Cunt sauce."

"Ladies," David said.

"Sorry, David," Bonnie said, "But she started it."

"What's Windows on the World?" I asked.

"Like you don't know," a fat girl with smudgy clown lipstick said. She was hugging a two-ton chrome makeup kit. "It's the club, up there ..."

She pointed to the top of the World Trade Center's North Tower.

"We're doing a photo shoot," Bonnie said, jiggling my face with a chest heave, pretending that it was just bad driving that was giving me a face job.

"Ten minutes to midnight," the driver said through the intercom.

When we got to the top of the tower after watching a hundred and seven elevator buttons light up, the place was in a happy, downward spiral. Peter Jennings was at the bar, sucking down tonic water straight from the bottle. A few seven-foot bouncers came out and cleared a path through the crowd so we could get to a cordoned-off space in front of a wall-sized picture window.

There was our crazy, twinkling city.

"What's the photo shoot about?" I asked the makeup artist, but then the deejay called two minutes and the place came apart.

Suddenly, everyone was dancing like they wanted their arms and legs to break. Strangers kissed. Drinks were poured into any mouth still open and empty. People came in their undies. You could tell by the somersaults their faces were doing.

"Quick, everybody in front of the window!"

LaChurch, the architect of New York's ugly beauty, wanted to capture his family on a once-in-a-lifetime background: the lights going out, the city's ugliest, most beautiful moment.

He was aiming a Polaroid camera, taking time to frame his masterpiece. No darkroom required, even though everything would soon be black.

"Listen," I said to David, "I want to talk more about the writing job."

"What?"

Tears for Fears' "Mad World" spawned a mini-riot.

"I'm a writer ... we talked about this?"

"TEN, NINE—"

"Oh, that," David said.

"SEVEN, SIX—"

He gave me a sheepish look.

"I was going to ask you to model for me. You write?"

"THREE, TWO—"

Fuck me. Derek's show was somewhere out there. But I was dreaming, right?

"ONE—"

My head is filling with impossible objects.

All this stuff I collect in my mind, the shit and ephemera and mislaid poetry, it's smashing together and tangling into new shapes that are meaningless to me.

I've built a world I can do nothing with.

Twilight. Grey migraine. So this was what morning felt like on the day the world was supposed to end.

I stumbled onto Wall Street and zigzagged through the skyscrapers, kicking through frozen-stuck piles of confetti, broken bottles, and sparkly plastic "Happy 2000" glasses, the ones where your eyes were the first two zeroes. Somewhere along the way, I realized that I was walking to the loft.

I had lost my keys, so I rang the downstairs buzzer. No answer. A delivery guy left the building and I slipped in behind him, taking the stairs two at a time. I had trouble finding the right floor because someone had ripped the number off the stairwell.

Knock-knock-knock-knock. Still no answer.

"Derek? ... Derek, it's me."

"I know who it is."

I lifted the corner of the mat, scooped the extra key, and turned it in the lock.

He was just standing there motionless, poring over a book.

"Listen, I'm sorry," I said. "I was going to be there, but David LaChurch asked me to write for him and then we—"

"Your excuses don't work on me anymore. Let me read something to you. It's from a delusional book by a delusional boy."

He was holding my notebook.

"I quote: 'Love. It's a weird word. But when the person in question is the only one down in your pit, down in the muck with you shoveling out a space to breathe, it's the only word that fits.'" He looked up at me. "Do you realize how ridiculous that sounds? It's the only word that fits? What love are you talking about? How I let you crash here, eat my food, and waste away? Do you think you're the first whore I've kept around like this? And if it was love, do you think I'd have registered the serial numbers of my electronics with the police?"

I refused to cry for this asshole.

"Go on, explain yourself," he said.

"You washed my cuts ... you painted them. And my bruises, too. We understand each other on a deeper level, and that's why we've never had sex, and we don't have to talk very much. We're like the turtles—we make art, and we just know."

My Fiorucci duffel bag, I could see, was packed and waiting by the door.

"And I've watched you create new colors, you fucking bastard."

"This fairy-tale romance of yours," Derek said, "is starting to make you look stupid."

He bent over, laid my notebook in the bag, and zipped it shut.

"I'm sorry," I said.

"Jaeven, you don't even know what you're apologizing for."

"For everything. I'm sorry I missed your show."

"Please leave."

Broadway and Houston. Feet dragging me to a building that wouldn't open up. Where was Phil when I needed him to need a massage from me?

I called him from a payphone.

"You have a collect call from ... state you name ..."

"Jaeven."

"Will you accept the charges?"

"Uh ... yeah. Hey ... what's up?"

Little pleasure groans punctuated his words.

"Happy New Year," I said, sniffling. "I thought you might like a massage."

"Well, I'm kind of getting one right now."

I heard shuffling, then someone else took the phone.

"Listen, asshole, he's through with you. You never knew how to get in under his muscles. He told me so."

I'd recognize Trey's snooty voice anywhere.

"And Phil and I agree that you're *so* last year. I'm the new Boy New York now."

Click.

I collapsed in a corner, where the sidewalk met a building, and propped my bag between my head and the concrete.

Stupid, but I wanted to write.

For as long as I could remember, writing was the only thing that could make the shit of life bearable. I didn't need anything else. The words would come and strangle the feelings, or rearrange them into something peaceful.

But Derek hadn't packed a pen for me. I had to go all the way to Fiorucci to get a new one.

I found myself today, torn out of a magazine.

I should submit it as a joke to Encyclopedia Britannica as the picture entry for "Physical Perfection," or maybe for "Temptation," or who knows what else the guys who clipped this photo thought it meant. Maybe "Doom." At the time it was taken, I'm not sure if the four-inch glossy spelled more doom for me, or for the guys who spent their days hunting the dork with the erection, running red lights, crashing into signposts, jerking off onto dashboards.

The photo. I'm not sure where I was and I forget who took it. I'm naked and spacing off, not really there. Maybe I should enter it under "Evaporation." Not in the bad way, the way where you disappear completely, but rather like floating, floating in the space past the magazine page.

Well, here, actually.

Tilting my Walkman at just the right angle, I can still get "Ordinary World" to play, though it's much fainter than before. There are whispers where there should be yells, missing words and washed-out choruses, and no matter how high I crank the volume, the wind smothers what's left of the song.

I used to think that no matter what happened, the music would always save me. I used to think a lot of things.

I got new batteries from Fiorucci and put them in my pager today. It beeped for the first time in a week. I recognized Richard's number right away. I called him back, and he told me to meet him at the Tony

Schafrazi Gallery, though he wouldn't say what it was for. Like I've done with him so many times before, I took a leap of faith.

The art world glitterati were being their usual selves—sharks swarming the chocolate fondue, all silver cufflinks and wine-stained teeth.

It was ridiculous to see Richard in public, in a suit jacket fiddling with the elbow patches, mingling with people who kept getting his name wrong. He looked relieved to see me.

"My God, hello. It's the year 2000."

He gave me a hug.

"Come on, put your bag down and stay awhile. I'll show you the pictures."

I don't think I could've prepared myself for what was hanging on the wall—I wouldn't have dressed any differently, I couldn't have avoided the feeling of being a stranger in my own skin, and I would've been equally shocked.

Richard positioned me under a giant photo of myself. I was sprawled naked on his hardwood floor, peeping at the lens through a telescope I'd made by rolling up my notebook.

"Look at your face. You're saying, this is me, this is who I am. So deal with it."

"That's me."

"Well, right," he laughed, "who else is it going to be? Come on."

In each of the photos on the wall, I was writing personal shit I'd never meant for anyone to read. Now here was a gallery full of people with their heads tilted, eyes squinting.

I walked around from photo to photo, rubbing the scruff on my face, sinking deeper and deeper into this museum of myself.

Sepia-toned shot of me propped up on an elbow, winking at the camera through the reflection in my herbal tea. I was expecting to read a gummy love letter about Derek, with paragraphs retraced over and over to make them real. Instead, I found a page about how photography had made me a real boy, and had given me so much more than it had taken away.

Shot of me upside-down with a pen between my teeth, holding the notebook up to Richard. I was expecting lines that were crooked and hopeless, showing the anger I felt because of falling for someone who couldn't love back, and who I was never going to have sex with. Maybe a few of the arguments I'd had with Derek, creatively rewritten so that I was the victor. Instead, I ranted about what a bad rap whoring's got, and raved about how close it could bring you to someone, if you knew how they constructed their distance.

Playful with my socks half off and tied together below the heel. I expected two pages of me gushing about Derek's color experiments and how he was chemically linked to Wink and Nod. Instead, I found reams of shit and ephemera, objects and substances that have defined this city for me.

Four shots of me curled in a fetal position on the carpet. Somber light. Four pages about why tapes are the best way to listen to music. You can always hear a whisper of the next song a half-second before it plays. You can tape over anything forgettable. Rewinding one side fast-forwards the other side. A tape ages like a fine wine.

Grainy shot of me shirtless, pensive, and drooling on the floor. Drawing a self-portrait, a crude semblance of myself, going catatonic over a notebook waiting to be filled.

"What do you think?" Richard said.

"Umm ... Wow. This has nothing to do with Derek."

"Right," he said. "You're fabulous. What I meant was, what do you think about being a published author?"

"I don't love you," I say.

Derek lets me in.

This loft, his place. I wonder if I'll ever be able to call it home. I'll try not to get too comfortable, and I'll even leave my bag by the door, in case he goes Protestant on my ass again.

It's so typical, Derek staring at me, watching me write, daring me with his eyes to verbalize what I'm thinking. The thing is, there's plenty to write but nothing to say. I guess it's my use of the word "love" that bugs him the most. I don't mind never saying it again. It's okay to be touchy about words, especially since they can do things to you.

Derek walks to the kitchen, pokes his head into the cupboard, and uncaps a bottle of olive oil. This means I'm going to eat well tonight. He chops up some garlic and throws it in the sizzling pan. The smell brings me closer. He adds some coriander and onions, and lights a match so he won't cry. His cooking routine calms me, and sends Wink and Nod into a happy waddle.

But it's no good. I've tried hard not to become starry-eyed, to believe that I deserve a lifetime of perfect and useless moments like this. I've learned, by now, how to recognize things that evaporate.

I tell Derek to put my dinner in the fridge, that I'm going out to get Burger King. Then I see that the Tupperware is already open and waiting.

There's still one lie I have to clear up with you. I told you that I don't write poetry.

My Walkman works today
and all is right in the world
it scares me
how precious life is
—this ebb—
when you only have one tape

I'm not sure what this list is for, but maybe you can help me sort it out:

Fuzzy dice, airplane wing tips, dominoes, toy trains, thumbtacks, pelicans, fish hooks, helium, Velcro lint, clown hats, teased hair, miniature castles, Debbie Harry's legs, tattoos that don't match, rat tails, whipped cream, pimp canes, car explosions, TV moms, milkshakes, water guns, ceramic leopards, blow-up dolls, paper lanterns, generic trophies, gold that turns green, fists, buttons that never fall off, baby's breath, diamonds, bourbon, art, peep-show channels, ice cream, inner tubes, animal masks, surprises covered in cereal dust.

ACKNOWLEDGMENTS

This book is the result of so many generous contributions.

Thanks to my A-Team of readers: Earl Brown, Tushith Islam, Sara Latini, and Jair Matrim for revealing the unexpected in the messy drafts I sent them, and Dave Lehman for tilling the microscopic so thoroughly.

Thanks to the firecrackers at Arsenal Pulp Press: Robert Ballantyne, Janice Beley, Bethanne Grabham, and Shyla Seller for guiding this book to publication so passionately, and Brian Lam for believing, and for his expert edits.

Thanks to all who helped us after the fire: Catrina Calcara, Janet Cox, Sheena Hoszko, Hicham Illoussamen, Farah Khan, Skye Maule-O'Brien, Marie Tilbe, and Jordanna Vamos for their outpourings of love and logistics, and Alex Boctor, Erin Harris, and Chris Hein for giving us shelter. These genius rescue efforts helped me stay focussed on the writing of this book.

Thanks to my supporters, guides, and confidantes: Francisco Ibáñez-Carrasco, George K. Ilsley, Bruce LaBruce, Derek McCormack, and Hal Niedzviecki for kicking ass and championing my stuff, and Mattilda Bernstein Sycamore for reality checks on the rigors of street life, and for making my work answer to the question "Why should I believe any of this?"

Thank you to Stanley Stellar for helping uncover the real 'me.'

And a special thank-you to Mark Harris, who has long kept my Coney Island dreams alive, and whose feedback, patience, and daily support have made Shuck such a wonderful ride.

Love,

DAC

DANIEL ALLEN COX is a former *Inches* cover model, video
porn star, and interviewer for the *New York Waste*. He is
the author of the novella *Tattoo This Madness In* (Dusty Owl
Press), and lives in Montreal.